# Passage To Dusk

Modern Middle East
Literatures in Translation
Series

# Passage To Dusk

## Rashid al-Daif

Translated by Nirvana Tanoukhi
Introduction by Anton Shammas

The Center for Middle Eastern Studies
The University of Texas at Austin

Library of Congress Catalogue Card Number: 2001091718
ISBN: 0-292-70507-7

Printed in the United States of America

Cover painting by Waddah al-Sayed, Damascus, Syria. Artist al-Sayed donated the painting to the Center in 1996.

Cover design: Diane Watts

Series editor: Annes McCann-Baker

The Center gratefully acknowledges financial support for the publication of *Passage to Dusk* from the National Endowment for the Arts in Washington, D.C.

With love and gratitude to Ghassan T. Tanoukhi, for early challenges in translation.

Nirvana Tanoukhi

## Map of Beirut during the Lebanese Civil War

**East Beirut**: predominantly Christian

**West Beirut**: predominantly Muslim

**Green Line**: artifical border separating Beirut's Eastern and Western sectors.

**No Man's Land**: an evacuated area, which was formerly "down-town" Beirut

**South Beirut**: a shanty town formed at the southern outskirts of Beirut during the war, populated by predominantly Shi'a Muslim families who fled South Lebanon.

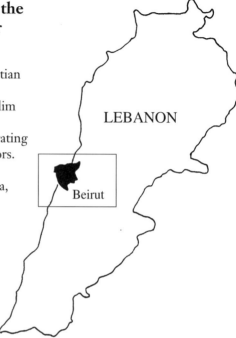

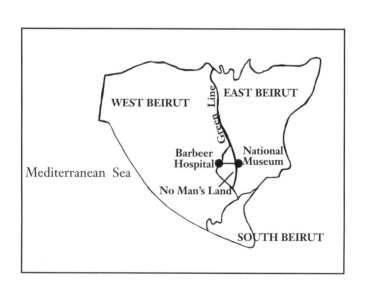

# Introduction

*Passage to Dusk*, the second novel of Lebanese author Rashid al-Daif (pronounced /ra-sheed ad-da'eef/), was published in Beirut in May of 1986, four years after the Israeli invasion of Lebanon and eleven years after the eruption of the Lebanese civil war, which ended, in some form or another, five years later in 1991. If nothing else, its playfully long Arabic title, *Fus`hah mustahdafah bayna al-nu'as wal-nawm* (literally: a targeted, or intentional, zone or space, in between drowsiness and sleep), is probably one of the most subtle, literary commentaries on that sixteen-year war. Beirut, the only city in which the novel could have been written, and whose cartography of destruction is inscribed onto the interiors of the first-person narration, was at the time divided by a "green line" into two sections: East Beirut—by and large Christian, right wing, and anti-Palestinian; and West Beirut—by and large Muslim, left wing and pro-Palestinian. But there were those few who, for various reasons, defied the dictates of ethnic loyalties and preferred to cross the lines, at more levels than one: Muslims who lived in the East and Christians who lived in the West.

Al-Daif was born in 1945 in Zhgarta, a stronghold of Maronite Christians in northern Lebanon. He lived in West Beirut throughout the war in that "targeted zone" between religious loyalties and political beliefs, as did a few other Christians from the leftist, secular camp. They lived at times under assumed Muslim identities, so as to protect themselves against kidnapping and other forms of reciprocal atrocities. Moreover, al-Daif's narrator, whose body throughout the novel, much like the city itself, is the target of physical attacks, real as well as imaginary, finds himself trapped in that space between drowsiness and sleep, where threats become visible and nightmares on a good day the stuff that daily life is made of. However, in the novel, that targeted space is constructed by language and within language, so for the narrator and the implied author behind him, language becomes the only reality. "It is a reality in language," al-Daif would say in 1999 about his novels, "but in a language that is built and structured, and the moment it is that, it is no longer an exact mirror of reality." (*Banipal*, 49)

Prior to *Passage to Dusk*, al-Daif had published two uniquely stylized collections of poetry and a novel, *Al-Mustabidd* (The Obstinate, 1983), which ends, to my mind, with one of the most memorable scenes in the literature written about the Lebanese civil war, and foreshadows by juxtaposition an important theme of *Passage to Dusk*. The narrator of *Al-Mustabidd*, whose name is also Rashid, is a college professor who is obsessed throughout the novel with the search for the true identity of one of his students, a young woman with whom he had the most fulfilling sexual experience of his life. (The novel has some of the most sexually explicit sections in modern Arabic literature.) The event took place during an Israeli air raid on Beirut in a dark, makeshift shelter, when the student accidentally sat on his lap, and he never made out her features. In his obsessively obstinate search for the woman, which spans the length of the novel, he recalls at one point being stopped at one of the many checkpoints in Beirut, "where they used to kill people *à la carte [d'identité]*," as the narrator comments. He had been kept in custody for three days at the checkpoint because he couldn't prove his "true identity" to the militia soldier in charge, who didn't like the fact that the other passenger in the car, a woman, belonged to a different sect. Nor could he prove the "true identity" of the friend whose car he was driving that day.

During the war, civilians were killed at checkpoints, because they belonged to a "wrong" political party or a religion (and there are seventeen officially recognized confessional affiliations in Lebanon); checkpoints became part not only of the urban landscape in the war-torn city, but more so of the deep structures of personal identities. One's identity wasn't defined by the rubric of "denomination" on the Lebanese identity card but, rather, by the person who happened to be checking that ID at the checkpoint and whether or not he would deem it valid and true. That's why Rashid in *Al-Mustabidd*, who is fashioned, as in most of al-Daif's novels, after the real author, tells the reader that he used to carry a false identity card, giving himself an assumed name and denomination as a protective measure against the whims of those who manned the self-proclaimed checkpoints into West Beirut.

Now Rashid frantically tries to follow a car in which he believes his lost student is riding. He drives his car through the streets of Beirut, consumed by the realization that this might be his last chance of finding out the truth about that brief encounter. And then he finds himself drawn to the same point where he had been humiliated a year before. But much to his surprise he discovers that the checkpoint has disappeared. True, there are some stones left, and the entrance to the adjacent building where he was kept in custody are still the same, but the checkpoint is nowhere to be found. He stops his car in the middle of the road, gets out and pulls out his identity card and, waving it in the air, shouts at the top of his voice: "Where is the checkpoint? I won't pass through until my identity card is checked." In the meantime, jammed cars behind him honk noisily, and drivers shout at him to move his car, but he goes on waiving his ID and insisting that the checkpoint should be there. Much to his fury, a passerby tells him that the checkpoint has been relocated. Then a person, clad in an army uniform, steps forward and introduces himself as the soldier in charge and asks for Rashid's ID. He hands it over to him. The soldier examines it pensively and re-examines it, then hands it back to him. "Go on, Allah be with you," the soldier tells him. Satisfied, he gets back in his car and drives away.

In *Passage to Dusk*, the narrator goes through a reversed variation of this theme: he is very reluctant when it comes to disclosing his real name when asked, lest his own name be used against him as a lethal weapon. His identity is first revealed to the reader through a casual reference to certain objects in his apartment, as they are scanned through the eyes of Abu 'Ali, the apartment superintendent, whose name would immediately be recognized by a Lebanese reader as a common Shi'ite name:

[Abu 'Ali] left that bedroom and turned to the kitchen, past my own bedroom. He stopped there for a while. He didn't go in, but did examine it with his eyes—every single detail: the collected works of Marx and Engels in a small set of shelves near my bed, a shelf of record albums... Exposed, one cover showed an album of Syriac religious hymns. The cover showed Saint Charbil kneeling before a large wooden cross. (p. 17)

The Lebanese reader would also recognize the fact that Marx and Saint Charbil, a secular mind and a Maronite Christian saint, are mutually exclusive constructs, and cannot be shelved comfortably together in a Lebanese house, let alone be examined by a Shi'ite Muslim in West Beirut. And the narrator, whose "real" name is disclosed in passing toward the end of the novel (but even then we are not sure whether or not it is really his name), becomes cryptic when he is outside the imagined—and now threatened—safety of his home. When he is taken to the hospital, after being injured by a shell and feeling that he might lose his right arm, he is extremely careful in answering the staff, who bombard him while he is in that targeted space between consciousness and unconsciousness with questions about his personal details. He doesn't know what hospital he is in, nor is he sure what side of town the hospital is in. And when they press him, he gives a neutral name that won't reveal his religion, his politics, or his region:

I was afraid of exposing my identity, of being murdered. Especially since I was on the verge of unconsciousness and couldn't make out the hospital or the region. I kept my mouth shut, knowing very well how easy it is for a wounded person to be murdered at a hospital...
They went back to their questioning and again I was afraid that the hospital might be in the Eastern

sector, and me a Shi'ite, or a Druze, or a Sunni, or a
Palestinian, or a leftist...
They went back to their questioning and again I
was afraid that the hospital might be in the Western sector, and me a Christian, or Maronite, or an
atheist, or a leftist. (pp. 49–50)

In *Dear Mr. Kawabata*, al-Daif's sixth, semi-autobiographical
novel (published in the beginning of 1995), the reader finds out that
that scene in *Passage* is based on a real life experience of al-Daif
himself. As a member of the Lebanese Communist Party living in
West Beirut, al-Daif was given a false identity card (along with other
Christian party members) during the first weeks of the fighting in
1975. He was issued the card by an armed Palestinian organization,
who gave him a Palestinian Muslim name—Muhammad Ayyub, a
Palestinian place of birth—Jaffa, and a Palestinian rank—fighter. In
the first years of the war he was badly injured in his right arm and
neck and was for a long time left bleeding in the street, suspended
between life and death, before he was brought to a hospital. He re-
members voices asking him for his name, as if it would acquire the
power to heal him immediately were they to know it. "As when the
electricity fails while you are in an elevator, and when you shout for
help a voice answers you from the outside: 'Who's there?' As if your
name is what would save you." At the hospital, and as the only survi-
vor, he is looked upon disdainfully by the relatives of those who
were killed in the same shelling, and he tries his best to stay conscious so that he is not mistaken for dead. Much to his horror, he
discovers that the number of the coffins brought into the room ex-
ceeds by one the number of dead bodies.

Al-Daif joined the Lebanese Communist Party in the late sixties
and, later, while in France preparing for his Ph.D. degree in literature in the mid seventies, the French Communist Party. In the early
eighties he was saved from certain death in Beirut because he was
late in getting back home from teaching: a booby-trapped car, which
he had noticed parked in front of his apartment building when he
had left in the morning and had secretly admired and coveted, blew

up seconds before he came back home, killing a PLO activist. He decided after the incident that Marxist theory was not applicable to Beirut reality in any shape or form. He told himself that he didn't need analysis and comprehension but, rather, "confession, screaming, and holding pain up in the face of recklessness." He had already left the Communist Party when he published his first novel, *Al-Mustabidd*, in 1983.

During the war years al-Daif discovered that language takes a course of its own, a course that has nothing to do with reality; that people are tools in the hands of a beastly, enigmatic, all powerful creature—history. Marxist analytical thinking, he asserts, was no longer useful to him, and what he needed was a confessional mode. So he "went back to literature," realizing that literature was the only means possible to "capture" the mercurial reality which none of the prevalent conceptions could grasp or make any sense of. Literature, he believes, is as mercurial as reality:

> In this sense, there's no doubt that the war had an influence on my writing; it was war that taught me evil is bottomless, and that humans have an unfathomable ability to inflict suffering on each other, and that they can't survive without an enemy, and that if they didn't have an enemy they'd create one out of themselves. War taught me that only literature can express this truth; in other words, it revealed the true significance of literature to me. (*Al-Adaab*, 81)

This view seems to be shared by some of the writers who emerged during the Lebanese war, a group that would primarily include Elias Khoury, Hoda and Najwa Barakat, Hanan al-Shaykh, and—from a younger generation—Rabi' Jaber. They have, respectively, introduced into modern Arabic literature, since the seventies, probably some of the most refreshingly daring yet fine-tuned styles of Arabic fiction. Al-Daif, the author of nine novels and three collections of poetry, is a writer who is constantly experimenting with the boundaries of literary Arabic and the ability of its margins to intersect with

Lebanese colloquial Arabic and with words and expressions in French and—more increasingly—English.

In 1998 al-Daif published his eighth novel, *Learning English*. The novel attracted attention not because of its autobiographical overtones—that had long been established as a main feature of al-Daif's work, nor because of its unusual openness in discussing matters that are taboo in first-person narration in Arabic literature—the mother-son relationship, nor because of its linguistic texture that, according to al-Daif himself, was his best stylistic achievement to date. Rather, what was curious about the novel was actually its title: a transliteration in Arabic of an English compound, an ironic comment of sorts on the perils and attractions of globalization in a society that still has to deal with blood vendettas.

Al-Daif's most recent novel, *Testfil Meryl Streep* (*To Hell with Meryl Streep*, 2001), is a monologue of a close-minded, hurt, and suspicious husband whose wife prefers to spend time with her mother, despite the 250-channel TV set he has bought for her enjoyment. Through an entertaining analogy between what the husband watches on the screen, most of which is in a language that he doesn't fully understand (including Streep's 1979 *Kramer vs. Kramer* performance), and the reality of his collapsing marriage (including extremely explicit sexual references), al-Daif manages to create a language of fiction in which he realizes his notion of the poetics of the unfinished form.

"At first, a building of stone looks more beautiful than a building of concrete," al-Daif argues, "and everyone seems to complain about what they call the 'forest of concrete' in our modern cities being the quintessential ugliness." However, for al-Daif, building in stone is similar to writing in the classical mode, as opposed to the concrete of free poetic language. In order to accommodate the masses, there simply aren't enough stones, so we need concrete, which is a democratic necessity, much as the novel is a democratic genre. For al-Daif, the concrete unfinished form, being a characteristic of Lebanese architecture, has its own poetics:

> Personally, I don't like the finished form much. I wouldn't live in a finished villa surrounded by a beau-

tiful garden, as we see in the Swiss countryside. Rather, I find delight in seeing a house whose roof has two pillars sticking out, with a clothesline strung between them. Then after a while the two pillars become four... and then they support a roof, which becomes in turn the shelter for the first sibling to get married, and from which two new pillars stick out, with a clothesline strung between them, etc... In this unfinished form of construction I can see the totality of life, while the villa projects a finality of sorts that depresses me. (*Al-Adaab*, 75)

Al-Daif's language itself, especially in *Passage to Dusk*, has its own poetics of the "unfinished form," as is evident in the unfinished, implied sentences; the fragmented consciousness which attempts to clutch at the equally fragmented, evasive reality through language; the narrating voice that feels the need, as well as the failure, to translate reality from the colloquial into literary language; and, above all, the unmade body which constantly mourns its phantom limb. In *The Man Who Mistook His Wife For a Hat* (1985), a series of case histories that deal with different neurological disorders, Oliver Sacks tells us that the sense of the body is given by three things: vision, balance organs (related to the auditory nerve in the inner ear which maintains the body's equilibrium), and proprioception, the sense which makes us feel our body as our own. In *Passage to Dusk*, the narrator feels that, much like his own country, he will never be able to regain that sense of proprioception. Still, Rashid al-Daif manages to create for us a proprioceptive text: it is language alone that can realize a phantom limb. And good novels, while doing that, are bound to give us great solace.

Anton Shammas
University of Michigan

8

## Endnotes:

In the writing of this Introduction I have drawn mainly on the following sources:

*Al-'Adaab* (Beirut), 47: 3-4, March-April 1999, p. 73-85. (A lengthy interview with Rashid al-Daif by Yusri al-'Amir.)
*Banipal* (London), Autumn 1999 (9), p. 48-49. (An interview with al-Daif by Margaret Obank.)
*Fusul* (Cairo), 16: 4, Spring 1998, p. 167-172. (A short paper by al-Daif, on the Lebanese novel.)
*Al-Naqid* (London) 4: 44, Feb. 1992, p. 64-65. (A short contribution by al-Daif in a special issue on "Cultural Capitals: Beirut.")

Two articles on al-Daif are recommended for further reading:
• Samira Aghacy, "Rachid El Daif's *An Exposed Space Between Drowsiness and Sleep*: Abortive Representation," *Journal of Arabic Literature*, 27: 3, October 1996, p. 193-203.
• Mona Takieddine Amyuni, "Style as Politics in the Poems and Novels of Rashid al-Daif," *International Journal of Middle East Studies*, 28 (1996), p. 177-192.

## Works by Rashid al-Daif
Novels:
1) *Al-Mustabidd* [The Obstinate]. Beirut, 1983.
2) *Fus`ha mustahdafah bayna al-nu'as wal-nawm* [Passage to Dusk]. Beirut, 1986.
3) *Ahl al-zill* [Shadow Dwellers]. Beirut, 1987.
4) *Tiqaniyyaat al-bu's* [Techniques of Misery]. Beirut, 1989.
5) *Ghaflat al-turaab* [Reckless Earth]. Beirut, 1991.
6) *'Azizi al-sayyid Kawabata*. Beirut, 1995.
   English: *Dear Mr. Kawabata*, tr. by Paul Starkey. Interlink, 2000.
7) *Nahiyat al-baraa'ah* [This Side of Innocence]. Beirut, 1997.
8) *Learning English* [Arabic title]. Beirut, 1998.
9) *Testfil Meryl Streep* [To Hell with Meryl Streep]. Beirut, 2001.

Poetry:
1) *Hina halla al-sayf 'ala al-sayf* [When the Sword Cut the Summer Short] / *L'été au tranchant de l'épée* (translated into French by J. E. Bencheikh). Beirut: Dar al-Farabi, Paris: Le Sycomore, 1979. (A bilingual edition.)
2) *La shay'a yafuq al-wasf* [Nothing Defies Description]. Beirut, 1980.
3) *Ayyu thaljin yahbutu bi-salaam* [What Snow Falls Down in Peace]. Beirut, 1993.

Fairytale:
'*Unsi yalhu ma'a Rita: kitaab al-baalighin* [Unsi Frolics with Rita: The Adult Version]. Beirut, 1983.

# Passage To Dusk

When he knocked on the door the first time, I was aware that he was late. I had already started wondering why he had delayed. What was his motive?

Then he knocked a second time before I could even cross the distance between where I stood and the door.

He knocked a third, a fourth time, again, a fifth time; then the knocking grew so insistent that I decided it must be someone else.

But who can this someone be and what does he want?

... I imagined the worst.

Could it be that someone had been watching the entrance and saw me coming in? How else could the person knocking have known that I'd come home after so long. When no one had seen me come in except the apartment superintendent, and when I hardly said hello to him in order not to be kept talking outside the building. I even interrupted him when he started asking me about my health and so on. I asked him to come up and see me in about an hour, after I'd rested, and he answered with his usual politeness, "Sure. In an hour. At your service."

It's been an hour and fifteen minutes and the super still hasn't shown up. Has he sent someone in his place?

And this knocking, it must be someone who's been tipped off about me, or someone who would rather I hadn't come back, who's come to make threats, or to kill.

And in either case, I have to answer the door.

In any case, I have to answer.

So I rushed to the door.

My chest was bare. I didn't put on a shirt or anything, even though my right arm was cut off at the shoulder.

I rushed to the door. To hell with indecisiveness.

I rushed to the door and opened it with my left hand. I took one step out. "Yes?" I called. And the rest I don't remember.

I was murdered on the spot. They must have killed me because I scared them. They were afraid of me, so they killed me. The super was one of them and he was the only one without a beard; the others had beards—trimmed, short, black, and full. They were all tall except for the super; and they all shot at me, including the super. But how can that be when the super was unarmed? It's a serious flaw in my testimony. I admit.

But I did see him with my own eyes.

I saw him without a gun, shooting at me. His bullets pierced me just like the other bullets.

I can still see it. The flame coming out of his AK-47. I can see it with my own two eyes. Why would I want to lie now that I'm dead?

He, on the other hand, has denied ever coming up to my apartment with anyone.

When the super knocked on the door the first time, I was aware that he was late. I had already started wondering why he was delayed. What was his motive?

My chest was bare, so I couldn't answer the door until I'd put my shirt on. When I finally got to the door, I wasn't sure he'd still be there. Because he knocked once and didn't knock again.

But there he was, waiting in the shade of the staircase. He wasn't holding a cigarette or anything else that implied he'd lost his patience. As soon as he saw the door opening, he started to walk in, without looking at me, without saying "hello," or "excuse me." So I got out of his way, and he walked in, straight into the living room.

I have a big living room—at least ten meters long. I've furnished it with only the bare essentials, so anyone can cross it from wall to wall.

Slowly, the super began crossing the room from wall to wall. Pacing. He took out a pack of cigarettes, Marlboros, from his jacket pocket, pulled one out, and put the pack back into his pocket. He waited for a while before reaching again for the same pocket, taking out a matchbox, pulling out a match, and striking it into flame. It flared, so he waited for the flame to subside and move from the match head to the stick. Only then did he light his cigarette, then shook the match twice in the air. When the flame went out, he looked around the room for an ashtray. Unable to find one, he kept it in his hand and kept pacing.

But the ashtray became necessary as the cigarette ash grew longer and was about to fall on the floor. Reluctantly, I went to the kitchen to get an ashtray. When I came back, I found him holding the cigarette with his right hand. His left hand, carrying the match, was poised to catch the ash about to flake from the ember. I put the ashtray onto the table, and the super, moving carefully, made his way towards it.

"Welcome, Abu Ali," I had said, as I cleared the way for him to come in.

Abu Ali bent down to tap the ash off his cigarette. Then he straightened up and started pacing again. He didn't say a word. It was up to me to say something to justify my asking him to come upstairs. But I had nothing for him to do. Why did I ask him to come up then? Why did I ask when I didn't need anything?

Why?

When Abu Ali sat down like a guest on the living room couch and when I found myself forced to chat with him as if he were a guest, I realized that whatever made me call him up to my apartment must have been of great importance. So once again I tried to think through what had happened. I had to figure out my motive.

I'm sure I wasn't carrying anything in my right hand, because my arm was severed at the shoulder. It had been blown off by shrapnel from an explosion before I reached the hospital. And I know I wasn't carrying anything in my left hand.

No one had seen me enter the building. I didn't see anyone at the entrance or on the sidewalk. None of the boys saw me either—the ones who usually gather next to the entrance, as if the sidewalk were the courtyard of their home. Them, I especially avoid.

I hadn't seen the owner of the fabric store across the street. He was probably busy with a customer. Well, at least I hoped so at the time.

The sun was to the west and the entrance to the east. But the sunlight, reflected by the windshield of a car parked there, lit up the entrance. I've never liked this kind of light. It makes me shudder. I feel it penetrating my eyes, penetrating my heart. It hurts me;

I break into a cold sweat. It is a distorted light. Utterly wrong. Nevertheless, I bore it with patience, responsibility, and strong will. I didn't hurry across the entrance hall. Instead, I crossed slowly as if I were coming back from work—just another evening.

Waiting for the elevator, I examined the super's door for a long time. Then I remembered that the electricity would be out at this time of day, according to the rationing schedule. That upset me. Such a mistake was unacceptable, considering the circumstances. Considering that I would surely have to pay the price for forgetting.

The super's door had been closed—unusual for that time of day. But the peephole was lit and light shone out through it, then it fell dark. Who could have been looking through? It must have been the super's wife because he leaves the door open when he's at home.

It must have been the super's wife bringing her eye up to the peephole, slightly above her eye level.

She is rising on her toes, lifting up her small body against the door. Her nipples touch the door. She stands, full-breasted, the small of her back curved.

Then the door opened to reveal the super.

"Welcome back."

"Hello, Abu Ali."

"I hope nothing..."

"Come up and see me in about an hour. I'll have gotten some rest by then."

If only the electricity hadn't been out. The elevator would have arrived in time for me to get in not fearing to be alone. I would've pushed the button, even before the door had shut (I won't mention the number, as a precaution). I would've gone up in the elevator without anyone seeing me, without Abu Ali surprising me by opening the door as I stood waiting.

I'd already remembered that the electricity was out, when Abu Ali told me. Frankly, I remembered a second before he opened the door. Actually, just a split second. But after he opened the door and after it all happened—the greeting and the unnecessary invitation to come up and see me—I forgot what I'd remembered. I forgot all over again, until he reminded me.

After spending over an hour in my apartment, I realized that I'd done the right thing, asking him to come upstairs. One of the shades in the living room was raised, and I couldn't pull it down. It seemed to me that it was broken, that fixing it would take a ladder and tools, and that to use tools it would take two hands. I only have one. The other one is always with me. We're inseparable. I managed to keep it close to me even in the worst of circumstances. Even when the shell exploded next to me, when the shrapnel pierced me and lodged in my flesh. Even then, like a drowning man grasping at air, I held onto two things:

My consciousness, which I wouldn't let go of for a second.

And my right arm. I pressed it with my left hand to its socket and held on to it. And I still do.

Abu Ali looked at the shade. Carefully, he looked it over and paused, seeming to detect the cause of the problem. He contemplated it for a long time, as if he were weighing his options. Then he left the living room. I couldn't tell where he'd gone, because a wall hid him from me. Alert, I turned my instincts to listening: he was moving to the right, towards the bedroom. Now, he was inside, opening the closet.

He bent down, reached for the toolbox on the floor, opened it, and took out the pliers and screwdriver. He stood up without closing the toolbox or the closet. He observed the clothes hanging inside and stopped at the jacket where I kept two weeks' cash, maybe more. Then again, he didn't know that—as far as I know, he didn't. He left that bedroom and turned to the kitchen, past my own bedroom. He stopped there for a while. He didn't go in, but did examine it with his eyes—every single detail: the collected works of Marx and Engels in a small set of shelves near my bed, a shelf of record albums... Exposed, one cover showed an album of Syriac religious hymns. The cover showed Saint Charbel kneeling before a large wooden cross. He couldn't tell if the person kneeling was a monk or a nun. That's why he kept staring at the drawing. It had to be obvious that it wasn't the picture of a saint on the wall, just a picture on an album cover.

When he reached the kitchen, he turned swiftly to the place where I kept my ladder. He picked it up, carried it to the living room, and put it down next to the curtain. Next, he put the box on one of the rungs. He walked to the ashtray, put out his cigarette, and set to work.

"The shade's broken."

"..."

"The spring is broken."

"..."

"I will try to lower it, but you won't be able to raise it after that."

"..."

"Did I tell you they tried to take over Saleem's apartment while he was away?"

I kept my mouth shut.

"And if I hadn't stopped them in time, they would have."

Again, I kept my mouth shut.

"I didn't notice what was happening at the beginning, because they were coming at night when the electricity was out. They were coming up and going down in the dark. It was my wife who first noticed them."

I heard a knock and moved to open the door, but he stopped me.

"No. Don't show yourself," he said. "Let me go see what they want."

Who the hell is *they*?!

He came down from the ladder, walked to the door, and opened it. He stepped out for a minute or two, maybe less—who knows? Then he came back alone, shutting the door behind him. He climbed the ladder again and managed to get the shade down, which I was never able to raise again.

"Six people," he said.

I rushed to the door and opened it with my left hand, without hesitation. I took one step out. "Yes?" I called. And the rest I don't remember.

I was murdered on the spot. They must have killed me because I scared them. They were afraid of me, so they killed me. He was there, the super. He was among them, one of them, and he was the only one without a beard; the others had beards—trimmed, short, black, and full. They were all tall, except for the super; and they all shot at me, including the super. But how can that be when the super was unarmed? It's a serious flaw in my testimony. I admit.

But I did see him with my own eyes.

I saw him without a gun, shooting at me, and his bullets pierced me just like all the other bullets.

"Six people who climbed the stairs whenever the electricity was out and came down while it was still out. No. Three of them went up and the other three stayed at the entrance. Then, the three who were upstairs would come down and they'd all leave together. I started watching them after my wife warned me about them."

At this point, he pulled down the shades. The shades came down and blocked off the outside, but light still came in through the other window—the one with the good shades.

After he came down from the ladder, Abu Ali put the toolbox, the screwdriver, and the wrench on one of the rungs. I stood up to walk him to the door, but he didn't move. Instead, he reached into his pocket and took out the pack of Marlboros. He pulled out a cigarette and put the pack back in his pocket. Instead of taking his hand out of his pocket, he fumbled busily with his fingers until he found the matchbox. He took it out, pulled out a match, and struck it on the closed box. It flared, so he waited for the flame to consume the head and move on to the stick. Then he lit his cigarette and shook his hand twice or three times in the air. He walked up to the ashtray, laid down the match, and sat on the nearest couch.

"I knew something was fishy, especially since most of the residents are Christian."

When he sat on the couch and crossed his legs, I had to follow and sit down in the chair opposite him, a little table separating us. It was the same table where I'd put the ashtray just a few minutes before, the one with the pack of cigarettes on it—a sealed pack of Marlboros.

I picked up the pack, opened it, and took a cigarette. Abu Ali lit my cigarette with one of his matches, put his matchbox next to the cigarettes, and settled back in his seat.

It was hot; it was twilight; the electricity was cut off and so was the water. The beginnings of darkness filtered dust into the beams of light from the window. The edges of the shadows blended into each other. My eyelids were becoming heavy and I was overcome by the need to sleep.

It was hot and humid. Sweat seeped out of my body. I was having to work hard to keep my eyelids from drooping.

"Many apartments have been taken over since they bombed South Beirut. But it's not the refugees who do it. It's a bunch of gangsters who take over houses and sell them to refugees for a lot of money."

When I first got home, instead of getting some rest, I spent my time checking whether everything was in its place. Nothing worth mentioning had been stolen. A spare bottle of gas for the stove, a bunch of *Playboy* magazines, a sheet of paper next to the radio with the names of radio stations, frequencies and times for different news broadcasts, and a brand new and very expensive transistor radio.

What bothered me most was losing that paper!

Could they have found something on the paper that incriminated me?

"It wasn't easy getting into your apartment. I spent a whole day in the basement looking for a key to your door. I tried dozens of keys and almost gave up, but finally found the right key. I asked a cousin of mine, who had fled the shantytowns of South Beirut, to come and stay here so that no one else would take it over."

I got scared.

"Poor guy. His brother was killed down in the shanties—shot by a sniper."

When the cousin had entered the apartment, I had blown out my candle and slipped into bed. When I heard him enter, I was as scared as humanly possible. The darkness was thick, and he moved around the apartment as if it were broad daylight.

First, I heard him slip his key into the lock, then he closed the door and moved toward my bedroom. And then he grabbed my left heel. I was sleeping on my stomach. He shook me and I sat up with a start. I didn't see anything except a bullet flashing at me from some point at the man's waist.

"His brother wasn't political. He was a watchman at a public school. He was twenty-six, married, had a son and a pregnant wife."

When I heard him slip his key into the lock, I stood up, scared. I went out and hid in one of the corners of the balcony. He looked for me all over the house and, when he couldn't find me anywhere, took off his clothes and lay down on my bed. He put his gun under the pillow. I spent the whole night almost naked on the balcony.

Luckily, it was hot.

"A few days after he was shot, a shell fell on his house and by some miracle his wife and child survived. His wife had to leave and I had to let her come stay with me along with her son.

"If only you could see how crowded my house has become. We sleep foot to shoulder. During the day, I ask the men to leave and not come back unless they have to. Only the women stay. But this can't go on, especially now that this woman and her son are here. She's pregnant."

When I'd gotten back home, I heard a strange stirring around as I opened the door. The sound was unfamiliar; I thought it came from the apartment next door. Then I realized it was coming from my own place. I closed my door without going in and went downstairs to the foyer.

I convinced myself that what I'd heard was only an illusion. Several times, I've gone into the house and thought I could sense some suspicious movements. Once, I felt someone in the apartment, waiting for me to sleep. I searched the place, looked in every nook and cranny, and, when the only thing left was the cupboard, I couldn't get it open. The sleepier I got, the more nervous I got. When I realized that I wouldn't be able to sleep without getting rid of my anxieties, I went to the kitchen and got a knife. I went to the armoire and opened it nervously with my left hand. Holding the knife, my right hand was ready to strike at the base of the intruder's stomach. I waited for a few minutes, and, when no one came out, I didn't laugh with relief. What hasn't happened to me has happened to others, and it would be my turn next time.

I went back to the apartment and opened the door, trying to forget about the noises, telling myself they were coming from next door. But no sooner had I closed the door than my eyes fell on a young pregnant woman, who froze when she saw me come in. She was obviously nervous and alone. Her boy was playing on the balcony.

I bit the inside of my lower lip.

She stood silent and I stood silent. She was young and pregnant and had a little boy who was playing by himself. Her husband had been killed by a mortar shell in the shanties. She was now in my house, and I could see her up close: she had her clothes on, her shoes on, a foot in each shoe. Then there was a knock at the door. She called her boy as I managed to bring myself to open the door, and Abu Ali walked in.

Abu Ali was saying, "She's due in a month and I have no idea how we're going to manage."

She was pregnant, but was slim as if she had been in her first month. She was full and firm, quick, cheerful, and familiar; she seemed so close you felt that you could almost touch her.

"I didn't want anyone staying at your place except my own relatives. I didn't give in to the pressure, even though it got pretty intense. Once, my dealings with the militiamen got so strained that there was no knowing what might've happened.

"They remembered that you weren't one of them and that you didn't belong here. What's more, they claimed you had a hand in some dirty dealings that you deserved to be shot for."

Who could've told them? Who could still remember that old story? It didn't even happen in Beirut.

I don't deny the incident. But I've changed, and so have my thoughts and convictions. I was young and reckless back then. How else could I have done what I did?

Who in his right mind would poison a spring to kill all the people in a village? It wasn't me who did that; it was that reckless boy who did it.

That day they had attacked a man from our village; they cursed his cross and the Virgin; they cursed Her; they raped the Virgin—that's what they did—and treated her like a whore! There's no name that they didn't call her, and they beat up the man and broke the gold chain that carried his cross. They trampled on the cross and spat on it, then went to the cemetery and broke all the crosses. They pissed and shit on the graves; they dug up the corpses and cut down the trees that gave shade to the graves, bringing them down on the bodies. And when the news reached our village, people went mad, lost their minds, old men were young again, children came of age, and women became fierce as predators, refusing to answer to their men until revenge was taken. As for the youth—and I was one of them—the news fell on us like thunderbolts, earthquakes, floods, and volcanoes, volcanoes of fire, of sulfur, spewing masses of lava… We didn't wait for the news to be confirmed and didn't wait to agree on a plan; we headed to the spring that watered their village, and I carried, along with some friends, a bag of poison so big that even a mule couldn't carry it. There was no problem getting the stuff; we just asked for it and it was ours. We emptied the bag in the spring that evening, the time of day they got back from the fields, to make sure no one would survive. They drank and slept and never got up. The fortunate ones who did not drink that night were finished off in the morning. We went there loaded with weapons, entered the village like conquerors; we snuffed out the souls of the survivors, destroyed the lives of the living. We spared neither fowl nor beast, left no tree standing, burned their crops and plowed up their graves; we burned and raised hell until the flames from their graves filled the sky…

I even went back alone that night, carrying a gallon of fuel oil. I crept into the reservoir from which the whole village drank. I poured the fuel oil in and went back, waiting for the news. It worked like medicine, cases by the dozen, nausea, vomiting, abdominal pains, diarrhea, headaches…

Yes!

That should teach them a lesson.

"If they said you deserved to be shot, they didn't necessarily mean they were going to kill you. But, I suppose one shouldn't take anything lightly these days."

It was hot, and I was so drowsy, I was practically asleep.

"When they tried to break down your door, there were five of them. Three stayed at the entrance and the other three went upstairs."

It was hot, and my body was so sweaty that it was difficult for me to move. A little darkness invaded the light in the apartment so that the shadows of things disappeared. It was quiet outside and the streets were empty except for a few people running errands which could no longer be postponed. The sound of bombing could be heard far away at the no-man's-land... Who would possibly bother to come all the way out here to kill me...?

I fell asleep.

I was so drowsy that I was practically asleep, so I went ahead and fell asleep. Perhaps then, if they came, they would think I was dead. I fell asleep, and when I woke up I was surprised to realize that I had slept with my eyes open... This meant I didn't have to open them with guilt and apologize to Abu Ali for being impolite.

"They said you belonged to some party. That you were right wing."

He had smoked a cigarette while I was asleep. I guessed that from the odd number of cigarette butts in the ashtray. If he hadn't smoked one, they would've been even, because we were smoking together. Whenever I'd take a cigarette, I'd hand him one, and he'd do the same for me.

He lights my cigarette first, his own second, then he puts his matchbox over my pack and settles back into his seat. Since we sat down, he hasn't smoked a single cigarette of his own. He hasn't taken one cigarette out of his shirt pocket.

I wonder what makes him feel so at home.

After all, our relationship is just one of tenant and super.

The cigarette ashes seemed darker than usual. I figured that it must have been the humidity; the ashes must have absorbed the water particles in the air, hardened, and become darker.

I picked up the ashtray to empty it, and he stopped talking. About time, I thought. He must be getting ready to leave. I spent as much time as I could in the kitchen, so that he would get the hint.

From the kitchen, I listened for any noises coming from the living room.

Listening for his movements, I realized that he was still there. He'd actually taken a fresh cigarette, lit it, and settled back in his chair once more.

When I stayed in the kitchen too long, he eased his rear to the edge of the sofa, reclining, almost lying down to keep from being uncomfortable as he waited.

Did he think I was making him a cup of coffee? Could he possibly be thinking that?

I had to get out of the kitchen then to keep his hopes from getting too high. I went out to the living room, put the empty ashtray on the table, and maneuvered my way back through the other rooms, checking them one by one.

The closet was still open. I reached for the jacket pocket and couldn't find the money. It's been emptied, I thought. Then I remembered that I had taken the money with me when I had left Beirut after the fighting flared up. I reached into my pants and counted the money there. A hundred and sixty seven liras. Not much.

I heard a knock at the door. I shuddered, panicked, froze. Gathering my wits, I waited for what was going to happen next. I couldn't see the door, standing at the closet. So I followed what was happening with my other senses. The super opened the door, closed it after a while, and went back to the living room where he put out his cigarette and started pacing again. After putting out his cigarette, he straightened up and moved away from the couch. I thought that he was leaving, so I almost called out to him.

I almost called out to him.

I almost called out to him.

I almost asked him to stay. But he was still there. He was pacing the living room. Up and down the length of the living room. Sometimes, he would turn right and pace the width. And, sometimes, he would turn back left and pace the length again.

The only choice I had was to ask him to leave. Otherwise, he wasn't going to.

"When they said you were right wing, I laughed sarcastically. 'Him right wing?' I said. 'You should've asked around some more before reaching that conclusion.'"

Who knocked at the door? Who asked? Who answered? Why hasn't he told me here in my own place? He's in *my* apartment and he knows it.

"These people know nothing about socialism. They claim to be progressive socialists when in fact they are reactionary confessionalists. As far as they're concerned, every Christian is backwards. They've taken over many houses with this excuse. They asked me about Fawwaz. He's a member of the Central Committee. They said he'd been behaving suspiciously. They asked about you too. They wanted to search your apartment to make sure there was nothing suspicious in it. They were looking for guns, communication equipment, and that sort of thing."

On that piece of paper, there was a list of radio stations and frequencies: 390, 1130, 1080, 1475, 990, 1274.

What did they make of that? They must've thought the numbers meant something. Otherwise, the paper wouldn't have disappeared. And the transistor radio, it's not a transmitter; it is a receiver but not a transmitter. And the *Playboy* magazines?

"I had two choices. I could either confront them or hand over the apartment to my cousin to live in and look after. So I handed it over to him... I never heard from you after that, and nobody told me you were going to come back."

When the young widow moved in, the tension between the super's cousin and me became unbearable. She moved into the spare bedroom with her son, and he wanted me to sleep in the living room because the bedrooms were adjacent to each other. Then he changed his mind. My sleeping in the living room would restrict their movement around the house.

It didn't take long for me to realize that I was supposed to stay out of her way. I had to make sure we didn't run into each other. I learned the rules quickly and acted on them. Whenever I'd go into my room, I'd lock myself in. Walking by the door and jiggling the doorknob to be sure it was locked became his new hobby.

One day, he bought a lock and installed it on the outside of the door. And every day, before going to sleep, he would lock it and put the key in his pocket. In the morning, he would unlock it, leaving the key in the lock.

Whenever he'd find any of my things outside my room, he'd grab them, open my door, throw them in, and slam the door shut—especially if it was my underwear.

Whenever I washed myself, I would make sure to take my soap and towel and everything that touched my body with me. I never forgot to clean the bathroom floor, dry the bathtub, and erase all traces of myself.

When I went to the bathroom to relieve myself, I'd open the small window and wait for the smell to dissipate, then return to my room.

But whenever I wanted to relieve myself when the water wasn't running and when there was no water left in the tank, well…

The plumber had advised me to throw the toilet paper in the wastebasket and not into the toilet, so that it wouldn't get clogged. But I couldn't leave such traces of myself. The price would be too high. Instead, I would put the toilet paper in a small paper bag and throw the bag into a wastebasket I set up on my bedroom balcony.

To be on the safe side, I got a pot in case I felt the urge during the night. I was lucky to have a balcony. I could put the pot out there after using it and cover it with cardboard. Each morning, after he opened my door, and after I'd made sure that he'd left, I would seize the opportunity and empty it in the toilet. If the water was running, I would wash the pot out before hurrying back to my room.

One day at noon, I opened my door to find a plate of food placed right there, at my door.

The living room was forbidden to me.

I ate the food, returned the plate to its place, and locked the door behind me.

Later, for reasons that did not escape me, he would open my door for only one hour. He would disappear into the room of his sister-in-law, the young widow, and come back in an hour to lock my door. In this hour, I had to see to my needs: first, I'd use the toilet, then I'd go to the living room and contemplate the objects there, then I'd go out and contemplate the world from the living room balcony.

The plate that she put the food on was clean. I had used it for special occasions. Silver. It was the same set that I had used for special occasions, the same spoon and fork and knife, the pinch of white salt on the small plate. (Is the saltshaker broken, then?)

The food was clean and smelled good, and the glass was full of transparent water, as if from a spring, and the loaf of bread was cut into four identical pieces. There were olives, carefully selected, mint, and a small onion cut in half.

One day, I got a paper napkin with lunch, so I wasn't given dinner.

It was time for dinner and the door was still locked. Dinnertime passed and still the door was locked. The weather was hot, the power was off, and the water wasn't running. The candle that lit my room had burned out, and I didn't have another. The mosquitoes were invading the room, but I couldn't shut the door to keep them out because the heat would have become unbearable. I would have drowned in my own sweat. I was forced to open the door and let the mosquitoes invade the room... I went out to the balcony but couldn't stay outside for long because someone could see me and think that the dead man's wife had someone living with her. I had to go back in, confused, nauseated, and throw myself onto the bed.

I threw myself on the bed because I didn't have the strength to do anything else. I wished I could fall asleep. But then the first mosquito arrived and hovered above my head. I shook my head right and left to keep it away. It moved away. So I returned to my fatigue and my desire for sleep. But it returned, followed by its sister. I heard them land on me. One of them came from the east and landed on my right shoulder, the other from the west and landed on my left wrist. I shook myself before they dipped their needles inside me and waved my left hand in all directions.

I did not resort to my right arm because it had been cut off and I was saving it for hard times.

I lay down again, returning to my fatigue and nausea, but again I heard their voices approaching.

Then there were three. Maybe more. I shook myself, this time flailing in all directions. But instead of escaping me, their determination grew, their numbers grew, and so did the violence of my flailing until I was exhausted and could no longer move. I finally surrendered because I couldn't hold out any longer... Then the mosquitoes threw themselves on me by the dozen. Each mosquito dipped its needle inside me and sucked all it could of my blood.

I was stretched on my bed, my right arm hidden beneath my torso. It seemed that thousands of mosquitoes were pouncing on me, as if they had abandoned the garbage heaps of the city, having found their long-hunted prey.

Each was the same. First came the sound of it, then it landed on me. Then dipping its stinger, silent, insistent, it drank.

When my skin was dried out, the mosquitoes were determined to drive holes deeper into my flesh to reach the moisture. And so it went—I don't know for how long—until my insides became a network of tunnels and passageways, a labyrinth where mosquitoes swarmed in search of water.

After my blood had been drained, after all my water had dried, it was the turn of crawling and creeping insects, especially ants. The ants disintegrated me and carried bits and pieces to every quarter of the city. There wasn't an anthill in all of Beirut without a shred of me in it.

But how?

How could I reassemble my self, recollect the shreds of me from the nests of ants, mice, cockroaches, rats, serpents, lice, and other vermin, spread throughout the city, whose hearts knew no mercy? The intensity of the fighting rose and fell, explosions were scattered along the no-man's-land, and if there was a second's pause, the next hour was even worse. Nobody could wander the streets of Beirut, especially me, because then they would suspect my presence here and put me under arrest. There are a thousand opportunities for opposites to meet.

No, I will not be the victim of any efforts to assemble my shreds.

I didn't pay much attention to the first two mosquitoes. I thought it was normal: two mosquitoes landing on me as I lay exhausted, time compressing, the electricity off, the water not running, the door locked, and my last candle burned out.

One of them bit me as I tried to lie down on the bed. Then I felt another bite. The rubbing alcohol was in the medicine chest in the bathroom.

The most painful mosquito was the one that flew into my nostril. I sniffed it in and started to cough uncontrollably. The more I coughed, the more mosquitoes I inhaled, and the more violent the coughing became. Finally, I managed to put the pillow over my head and push my mouth and nose into the sheets. I wished I could scream, call out to the husband's brother, or the wife's brother-in-law, or the super's cousin.

I gave up on survival that night and realized that it was the end. My only consolation was that my death wouldn't serve as an excuse for anyone, nor would it be a burden. There would be no need for revenge or for a reprisal kidnapping. There would be no need for a burial service. My body was already scattered.

The next morning, according to schedule, he unlocked the door. But how could I get up without a body?

At noon, I heard the plate being placed at my bedroom door. But how could I eat with dozens of mosquitoes swimming around in my saliva?

In the afternoon, I heard their questions drumming through the house. Then they made up their minds to call out to me. They did. I didn't open the door. I didn't answer. Again, questions were asked; then I heard a sharp tool being applied to the door. They came in: the super's cousin, the super, and the young widow who had stayed in her room. They couldn't find any trace of me on or beneath the bed, in the closet, on the balcony, on the sidewalk—anywhere.

But when they turned me over onto my back, they could see my front side. All that was left of me was my front side, thin as a pencil sketch.

He's dead.

That's what they said.

They put me into a small plastic bag and took me to the nearest police station. They submitted this as concrete evidence that I'd died a natural death, resulting from some kind of accident. Then they handed me over to the Red Cross, who handed me over to the Red Crescent, who handed me over to my family.

But my family couldn't believe that *he* was me.

They decided that I'd been kidnapped. And they decided, accordingly, to kidnap someone else or more than one person. That way, there'd be an exchange and I'd be set free. That was exactly what I had been afraid of. Because if they kidnapped somebody, that person's family or militia or sect was going to kidnap me and, with me living among them, kidnapping me could be the easiest thing in the world. So things became very complicated, so complicated that I no longer tried to understand them. I let go.

When they took me out of my apartment in that plastic bag, the dead man's wife felt sorry for me. But her brother-in-law was relieved. A weight had been lifted off his chest. Now he could walk around the house with a bare chest and bare legs. He started sleeping in my room, on my bed, and covering himself with my blanket. He would yell at his nephew, and sometimes he would beat him. At other times, he would pamper the kid, so that he'd stay on the balcony when he was around the house.

Then he started to raise his voice at his sister-in-law. He scolded her whenever her food wasn't to his liking, if she forgot to wash a shirt of his, if she went out without a valid reason, or if she went out with a valid reason but stayed out longer than he thought necessary.

He was generous with her, showering her with presents whenever he could afford it, even though she was the one with the larger income. She got a thousand liras from a certain militia plus her husband's salary from the Ministry of Education, since his death hadn't been officially reported.

He told her that he was obliged to her because he feared God. He said that he wouldn't leave her alone to suffer. And he said that he would give her everything her husband had provided, except what God had forbidden.

As for the young widow, at first she thanked him and asked him not to inconvenience himself because she didn't need him. But later she started raising her voice to him.

Then they started yelling at each other and he started beating her. So she'd get afraid and keep to her room, coming out only if she had to or if he was out. And she often remembered me.

Surely, she wished that he would leave us alone. I am a different kind of man, and, besides, it's my house. I might have wanted her to stay, and she might have wanted that too. She looked at me now, trying to contain her love for me. She was sad that I'd died.

One day, he accused her of wanting me. He threatened to kill me and to tell their cousin, the super, and her brother, the militiaman. Their yelling got louder, but she seemed to be hesitant. She must have loved me. She tried being sweet with him, so he calmed down, thinking that she'd make a few more concessions. He was in her room and the kid had awakened, so he asked her to go to the living room with him, to let the kid sleep in peace. They moved to the living room, him walking behind her. She suggested that they go out to the balcony, because it was very hot. He refused, saying that the balcony wasn't safe from the shrapnel of stray shells. It was hot and dark. The electricity was off, and the water wasn't running. A dim light came from a cloud, a candle lit in the opposite apartment, or a gas lamp. He was suffocating in the heat, he said, taking off his cotton shirt. He asked her whether she was hot. She said that yes, she was, but he didn't ask her to take anything off.

A little later, he said for her to put her nightgown on to cool off a bit. So she went to the bedroom to put her nightgown on. A few moments later, after enough time had passed, he followed her. Quietly, he swung open the door she had closed behind her, so the kid wouldn't wake up. "I'll make a jug of lemonade," he said before she could react. Her calves and thighs were visible beneath the short white slip. For a second she froze, wanting to get her dress back on, but he'd turned around and walked into the kitchen, leaving the door open behind him.

At that moment, she wanted to tell me something, but she couldn't. She was afraid that her brother-in-law would guess what she was thinking, so she stopped.

They went back to the living room. She was in her nightgown. His chest and thighs were bare. They were silent for a long time. He smoked a lot and she didn't smoke at all. She said she wanted to sleep, and he seemed amazed that she would. "How can you sleep in this heat?" he said, "Besides, it's still early. It's not even ten yet. They're still shelling. Wait a little till it gets cooler, and maybe the shelling will stop, then you can sleep soundly."

When he realized that she wasn't responding, he went straight to the heart of the matter. "They tell me that you're planning to get remarried," he said. She denied it, and demanded to know who could have made up something like that, but he avoided her question. He'd found a way into the conversation as he'd intended.

But he couldn't coax her in that direction, and when he started
to despair, his voice began to rise. But her voice also rose. He accused her of planning to get married and demanded to know what
would happen to the kid, and the baby in her belly, and the house
and the land in the village, and other things. This time, he even
mentioned the name of the man she'd intended to marry. I don't
know the man. I know nothing about him. As for her, she denied
it, and he became angry. She kept denying it, and he became an-
grier, and it could have turned into a huge mess, but he put his
clothes on and left. She got up after him and locked the door. She
left the key in the door and turned it a little to the right, or to the
left. After making sure that he couldn't open the door and take her
by surprise, she walked towards my door and knocked. I tried to
open the door but couldn't. Her brother-in-law had left with the
key in his pocket. Desire burned in me, and desire burned in her,
but the door stood between the joining of our desires. Our desire
couldn't burn the door down. She didn't say anything—not a word.
Instead, she leaned her shoulder against the door, then went back
to her room, where she lay down on her bed. She lay down for a
long time.

At dawn, her brother-in-law returned. He slid his key into the
lock, but the door wouldn't open. He turned it right and left; he
shook the door, but in vain. She woke up but didn't let him in. She
made him knock first, so he did, and she answered. "Why did you
lock the door and turn the key?" he asked. His question was filled
with suspicion and no answer would satisfy him. But he couldn't
make any accusations about me or her. My door was locked and
the key was in his pocket.

"Why did you lock the door?" he asked, and nothing could ease
his doubts.

"This mute man living with us must be up to something. No
matter how much I try, I can't understand him. How was he able to
cross the green line dividing our city, for instance? Why did he risk

his life? And why did he return before things settled down? Why, when the whole country is balancing in the palm of a demon?"

I had crossed the no-man's-land into West Beirut after passing the last checkpoint at the Museum gate on the way to Barbeer Hospital. Many taxi drivers stood waiting for customers: "Taxi?" "Taxi, Sir?" "Where to, Sir?"

But I didn't want to take a cab because I didn't want to attract any attention.

I thought it better not to carry anything in my hands. It would tell whoever was watching that I was going back to my own house, my own district, that I'd been there to run an errand and hadn't stayed there for long—just enough time to take care of something pressing.

When I reached the taxi station, I didn't hail a cab. I kept walking.

I walked a long way through the outskirts before reaching the center of West Beirut and blending into the crowds. I became a pedestrian among pedestrians. No one could have picked me out from the others—no matter how strong his instinct for stalking.

Walking, I watched the taxis passing. Many taxis with one or more vacancies drove past. But I didn't hail any of those because all of the passengers were men. I was looking for a car with a woman. To me, that meant safety. And so it was. A taxi approached with a woman in the back seat and a man in the front seat, next to the driver. I hailed that one and got into the back seat, leaving a space between the woman and myself. I was surprised.

When I had climbed in, I was surprised to find that the woman was dressed in black. A relative of hers must have died in the most recent fighting. It must've been her brother or son or husband, and it must've happened not long ago. A few days maybe. Her black clothes were new, smelling of unwashed fabric. The color unfaded, the creases intact.

Sadness had left that woman with an air of well being, despite the dark circles under her eyes. She was young and pretty, tall but not skinny.

I say this, though I didn't really look at her. I was able to steal a glance at her as I got into the cab and settled into the back seat.

I guessed she was somewhere between twenty-five and thirty. A good age.

She'd lost a man, for sure; she'd lost a man. Her mourning was for a man, not another woman. Everything about her testified to that.

As for the driver and the passenger sitting to his right, they didn't interest her. I couldn't feel an invisible current running between her and either of them. But it did run between us—me and her, her and me.

She didn't look at me. I didn't expect her to. I didn't look at her either, but she felt me and I felt her. Then she remembered the husband who she had just lost, and whom she missed, and she remembered her position and mine. Her body signaled to me in ways even an illiterate could read.

The front passenger was resting his hand on the arm of the seat. His skin was thick and cracked. Looking at his hand bound us together. My hands were soft, never having touched a rock or a hammer.

The taxi stopped for two young men of around twenty-five. "Where to?" "Hamra." They got in – one in the front and the other in the back, next to me. So I was pushed close to her. We almost touched. I was afraid the invisible current would change direction, but it only intensified.

Now I was in the middle. She was to my left, our clothes touching.

When the passenger had climbed in and I moved over to make room for him, she didn't move. She stayed in her place as if we were still alone on the seat.

The heat was intense and the street was packed with cars. It was noon, and it seemed that the sun would split the roof of the car. Sweat glistened on our foreheads and temples. Everyone was quiet. None of us opened our mouths, even to grumble. No one even talked politics—not a word. At some point, the driver tried to find a news broadcast on some private radio station, but couldn't. He lost interest and turned it off.

I was relieved.

The driver was old. Almost sixty or maybe even older. With men that old, you never can tell what they're going to do next. And that paradoxically reassured me.

The two young passengers seemed to be in some militia or another. Any talk about politics would have been risky. I was relieved.

I was also relieved because none of them knew me or anything about me. No one, whoever that someone might be, can tell a Muslim from a Christian by their skin.

No one had seen me cross the Museum checkpoint. But I was worried anyway.

The cause of my concern was the woman sitting next to me. It seemed that she could read me.

I was afraid that she might look at me, that I'd break down, that I'd pass out. She could blame me for the death of her husband.

That I was the one.

That I was the sniper, the man who fired the recoilless artillery, or the mortar, from a mobile—or immobile—missile base.

That I was the one who tore his body into shreds and stole from her the happiness of years to come.

"Stop," she cried suddenly, and the driver stopped. He turned to look at her, and so did everyone else in the car, except for me.

Instead of looking at her like the rest of them, I fixed my eyes in front of me. My thoughts lost focus, consciousness slipping away into nothingness. I could no longer hear or see or feel. My breathing stopped. My pulse stopped. It got to me. I'd… How shall I put it? I'd gone.

A slap woke me up.

When she had tried to step out of the car, she was yanked back into her seat. I was sitting on her dress. Unable to be pulled out of the car, the dress was hiked halfway up her thighs, or more. Her stockings reached just above her knees. After that, the flesh was white and bare, downed with light hair. Tiny pimples were barely visible in the sunlight.

I didn't look at her bare skin like the others. They stared shamelessly, while my eyes were fixed in front of me.

After freeing her dress from under me, she got up and out of the car in one motion.

"Pig," she said.

I don't know exactly when she said that. But when she did, I didn't turn toward her, so that she wouldn't look into my eyes and through them into my secret.

"Pretends he doesn't know what's going on," she said.

And she jumped at me and bit me, tearing out chunks of flesh with every bite.

"You won't get away with it."

She pulled my hair with her right hand, and pulled my head towards her. She stared with her eyes into mine. I shut mine immediately. But it was too late.

"Go ahead and shut them, you bastard."

I broke down. I collapsed. I was spent. I'd turned to ashes. Shreds of a corpse.

I didn't utter a word.

What could I say? What could I have said if I'd spoken? Wasn't it I who had done it? Or was it my brother? It was my brother, and that man happened to be her husband. Why should I pay for another man's sins? If I'm guilty of anything, it's keeping my mouth shut when I knew about it. But who was I supposed to tell? Where? And what? I didn't know him. I didn't know his name. I didn't know anything about him. I didn't know what had happened, what would happen, the motive, or the intention.

I'd read about it in the papers.

I learned about it from the papers, and my doubts led me to my brother, even though the papers didn't mention the name of the killer, his job, or describe him in any way. The only thing they mentioned is that the body belonged to a man in his thirties, found by the Beirut River, and that the coroner who did the autopsy decided that the man had been dead for twenty-four hours. He said that the corpse bore evidence of blows from a sharp object and burns in the shape of crosses. The papers didn't mention the last line in the doctor's report because the political mood was optimistic and they didn't want to do anything to reverse this trend.

"I'm going to drink your blood, you pig, you dog."

Why am I the dog? Why am I the pig? And why does this beautiful woman want to slash my throat? To fill a cup with my blood and drink it?

How is it my fault?

I only learned about it from the newspapers. From the newspapers I learned that the body, found a week earlier at the Beirut River, had been identified by the parents, that it was the body of this woman's husband, that he had been kidnapped a year, six months, and a day earlier, and that his kidnapper—the newspapers hadn't mentioned that he was my brother—had imprisoned him all this time, then murdered him.

The papers didn't mention that he was imprisoned merely as a precaution.

My brother had a son who worked in a bank on the Street of Banks, next to Riad Solh Square. Of his four children, he was the only boy. He feared for his son's safety, especially from kidnappers, and he tried to find him a job in East Beirut, but couldn't. So he decided to kidnap a man, just in case.

One day, his son didn't return home on time. There were snipers at the green line and at the Commercial Center where he worked. There was also occasional shelling at the front lines—but not in the residential districts. The father's heart burned. It was six o'clock and he hadn't returned. He'd phoned some of the employees at the bank to ask after his son. They replied that they'd seen him get into his car as usual after finishing work at two o'clock. The father lost his head. He grabbed his AK-47 and drove to the Museum area. He parked his car and watched the traffic coming and going. It wasn't long before he found a valuable catch: the unfortunate husband of the woman in mourning. He was alone in his car, on his way back from Tripoli. The father pulled the man out of his car at gunpoint and locked him in his trunk. Then he took him home, alive, and waited for news about his son.

He held the man in his house for a year, six months, and a day, during which time he gave him food, drink, clothes, and shelter in his son's room.

He had him eat what his son would've eaten, drink what his son would've drunk, and dress as his son would've dressed.

He held him captive in his son's room.

He did all of that so the man would know that holding him was not a whim or an injustice, that he wasn't a criminal.

During the imprisonment, many crucial events took place: the Israeli invasion, two presidential elections, the 17th of April agreement, and the February troubles.

After February, the father gave up on ever seeing his son alive. He decided to kill his prisoner, but he couldn't do it himself. So he handed him over to a man who'd survived a massacre in which all his family had been killed. The man took the prisoner thankfully and tortured him, slowly, for a whole week, until he died. Some say he mourned his prisoner's death.

All of this happened without my knowledge. I swear by all that is Holy, I'm telling the truth. I didn't know any of this, much less that my brother could be capable of it. Even now, after all that's happened, I'm not sure that it was him. I can even go one step further: I believe he's innocent.

And suppose he is guilty, how would that be my fault?

But God—no not God, Justice. Justice, unlike falsehood, gets bored. It didn't occur to any of the passengers in that taxi that I might have been the brother of the killer. They didn't make any connection between the mourning clothes of the woman and the murder. They actually stood by me.

"She's too snotty," they said.

The taxi approached my building, but I didn't get out. It was only after a hundred meters that I asked the driver to stop. I got out and stood waiting for the taxi to disappear into the traffic before walking back to the building.

Even though the taxi approached the entrance to my building, I didn't get out. When we reached Hamra Street and he asked where I wanted to get out, "The University Hospital," I answered briefly. He complained that this would take him off his regular route. I said that I'd pay him anything he wanted. I was getting worse. I was hemorrhaging at the shoulder. My arm was severed at the root. The passengers complained at first, but they felt sorry for me when, with their own eyes they saw the blood, my growing pain and pallor—that I was on the verge of dying.

But in spite of the pain and the shaking, I didn't forget what had happened between me and the woman in mourning. Even as I hemorrhaged, I was troubled about the coincidence of getting into the same car as her. Was it really coincidence? Or was it carefully planned? If it was coincidence, how did the super know that I was coming? He'd waited for me secretly on the Barbeer side of the Museum checkpoint.

He was waiting in a car with the woman in mourning, not very far from the last checkpoint. He couldn't have not seen me when I crossed that checkpoint. He was waiting for me, and so was the woman. He pointed to me, and she got out of the car and followed me. When she saw me watching the taxis, she realized what I was thinking. So she hurriedly hailed a car, the one I later got into.

The super was following us in another car, driven by a young man. It was the same car he'd waited in near the Museum.

After the woman in mourning got out of the car, after the incident between us, the super's car kept following us. At the time, I didn't know whether the super knew what had happened to me between the Museum and Barbeer. Because, when I reached Mansour Palace, the temporary location of parliament, I thought that I was safe, far enough from the Museum area and close enough to Barbeer.

The echoes of intermittent gunfire sounded in the area. It came from the center of Raas al Nabi', adjacent to the Museum district.

The bullets didn't reach me because I was walking like a man in perfect health. The bullets didn't reach any of the other pedestrians, nor the passengers in the two neat rows of cars: one going towards the Museum, the other towards Barbeer.

Whenever I'd hear a shot, I'd look at the people around me, make sure everybody was still walking, and walk on. But every shot made me want to cross the remaining distance more quickly. I'd start to run, then stop myself. I was afraid of arousing alarm, or suspicion. Afraid I'd look insane.

They told me later that when I arrived at the sidewalk opposite Mansour Palace, a shell exploded and the shrapnel hit me. The truth is, I didn't hear anything at all.

I didn't see the shell falling. I didn't see the shell exploding. They told me about it many hours later.

They said that it had killed five people, that one of them was a pregnant woman in her ninth month. They said it injured thirty pedestrians and motorists, that it came from the east and from the west. They said a lot of other things too.

Except for the falling of the shell, the explosion, and the damage, I remember everything that happened to me, within me, and around me. First there was a discomfort, very sharp, somewhere in the region of my right shoulder. I tried to ignore it, thinking it was a passing thing. I waited for it to gradually go away, but it became unbearable. I fell on the street near the sidewalk, not far from the gutter. But I was conscious when I fell. I can say with confidence that I did not fall. I just had to sit down.

The pain is still growing.

I felt my arm free itself from me, fleeing into the distance. I ran after it. But I was wounded, and my wound was bad, so I let myself fall to the ground. My arm came back to me after its fear had passed.

I was bleeding. My blood flowing over the asphalt.

I longed for it to flow into the soil of distant meadows, away from that asphalt, which is never thirsty and is never quenched.

I longed for my blood to water a fallow land, to make it bloom bountifully, reviving national anthems with new life and meaning.

But my blood ran over clenched asphalt—impenetrable. It ran towards the edge of the road into the mouth of the gutter, disappearing into the darkness. The rats went into a frenzy, emerged from their holes and started lapping it up. Being fond of thick sauces, they raced towards the source of it until they reached my shoulder. I moved my arm, but it didn't move. At that moment, I'd forgotten that I had another, a left arm. It had completely escaped me. My mind had slipped away from it, and my right hand wasn't complying.

It was humiliating, to have my blood lapped by rats.

It was humiliating to have rats reach my shoulder before someone could offer me a hand, before someone could save me, move me to a hospital, a clinic, or a house—anywhere other than this place which separates combatants, or rather, brings them together. I waited for a long time. But nobody came. How I wished that some human being would come up to me before I died. But no one did. So I got up, carrying my wounds, rising above the pain. I did it for myself, not to spite anyone and not for anyone else's sake. I walked on towards Barbeer.

When I reached Barbeer, no one asked me what was wrong. It was obvious.

When I reached the hospital, I was practically unconscious. I didn't know what hospital I was in. So I was careful answering the questions they asked me, because I wasn't sure which side of the city I was in. I was careful not to give any information that would reveal my identity. I didn't fall into that trap. They asked my name. I gave them one that didn't reveal my religion, my politics, or my region. They asked me where I was from. "From Beirut." "Where were you born?" "In Beirut." "Where do you live?" "In Beirut." "What do you do?" "What's your mother's name?" I told them my mother's name. "What's your father's name?" My father's name, again, didn't reveal his religion, his region, or his politics.

I was afraid of exposing my identity, of being murdered. Especially since I was on the verge of unconsciousness and couldn't make out the hospital or the region. I kept my mouth shut, knowing very well how easy it is for a wounded person to be murdered at a hospital.

When they realized that this questioning wouldn't make me reveal my identity, they resorted to another method, which they thought would be more effective.

They took my right arm from me.

If they'd taken my left arm, I wouldn't have cared. I'd forgotten all about it. I was thinking only of the other.

I couldn't even feel my left arm, only the right one.

When they tore off my shirt, they discovered that my right arm was severed at the shoulder. My shirtsleeve was the only thing keeping it in place.

They used it to pressure me; they didn't have to admit it. But who needs their admission?

It was obvious.

It was so obvious, it was crystal clear.

They said they were going to bury it because there was no hope of reattaching it.

They were dressed in white and were unable to understand that my desire to keep it had nothing to do with wanting to reattach it.

The hope of reattaching it was of no concern to me. None at all. I'm not concerned with the hope of it. Hope itself doesn't concern me. My only concern is my arm, just my arm. I want to keep it, and it doesn't matter if it's connected to the shoulder or not.

Leave my arm alone.

I told them as much. I screamed at them to leave it at my side. But I couldn't talk. I tried to talk with the last bit of energy I had left.

They went back to their questioning, and, again, I was afraid that the hospital might be in the Eastern sector, and me a Shi'ite, or a Druze, or a Sunni, or a Palestinian, or a leftist.

They went back to their questioning, and again I was afraid that the hospital might be in the Western sector, and me a Christian, or a Maronite, or an atheist, or a leftist.

They went back to their questions and again I answered with secular names. I was on the verge of unconsciousness and didn't know the hospital or the region. I kept my mouth shut, knowing very well how easy it is for a wounded person to be murdered at a hospital.

Then the super came back to me.

What if he followed me here with the woman in mourning? What if the two young men are working for her and drag me to an out-of-the-way place?

It must be the super's plot. He's the only one who knows I'm the brother of the man who—and I guessed right. The woman did give the orders. The two young militiamen, each armed with an AK-47, dragged me to the cemetery, where a number of martyrs had been buried.

The woman had set up a tent there, and the same two young men stood guarding the entrance—sure proof that the whole thing had been set up and prepared by the woman, these two young men, and especially the super.

The tent had enough room for at least fifty beds. I was in there alone with two blankets. I put one beneath me, and with the other I covered myself when it got cold during the night.

The entrance to the tent overlooked her husband's mausoleum. Every morning, she'd come to the cemetery and cry at her husband's grave. At the mausoleum door, she would kiss something that might have been a cross. She would sob, burst into tears, slapping her face and beating her chest. Then she would let her hair down, yanking at it as if she wanted to tear it all out. Then, suddenly, she would stand up, trying to regain control of herself. Calm again, she would turn around, walk into the tent, and approach me. She would crouch at a short distance, stare angrily at me for a long time, then walk out.

At dusk, she would come back and do the same thing.

I don't remember how long this situation lasted, but I remember that there came a day when I couldn't bear it any longer. I decided to make a change, to free myself from this hell, regardless of the consequences.

And so, one evening as she crouched before me, I sprang at her, not knowing whether to rape her or strangle her.

Rape would do more to provoke the guards.

I sprang at her, deciding to rape her. It had been a long time since I'd been with a woman… I got on top of her. She resisted. I covered her mouth with my hand to keep her from screaming. After a struggle, I was able to pull up her dress. I reached down to remove the final barrier, but she resisted stubbornly.

My left hand was on her mouth. So was my right. But she tore her mouth free and screamed, alerting the guards. They saw what was going on, with their own four eyes. But I didn't get off her until they dragged me off. Her dress was up around her waist. So she got up and covered herself. "He tried to kill me. The dog," she said.

I was about to explain, "Actually, I was planning to rape her." But she sprang at me and slapped me, leaving me with a bloody lip. Blinding me for a second.

I saw stars.

I tried to slap her back, but one of the guards dropped me with one shot. He hit me in the shoulder, where it joined my right arm. And although I didn't hear the gunshot, I saw the fire coming out of his AK-47. My legs would no longer support me. I had to make an effort not to fall, then I made an effort to fall slowly.

I remember her asking them to leave. They left.

She stood there alone before me, her belly swollen. She was pregnant. She'd gotten pregnant before her husband died. No man had come near her since his death. So, after she lost him, she started hating men. Perhaps this was made worse by her pregnancy. My fear of her grew with every visit, every time I saw the growing curve of her belly.

Her belly grew more rounded. The way she looked at me changed. Her behavior changed. Even the way she mourned her husband at the grave changed. She had used to cry like someone cursed. She used to roar like an animal raging for its mate in the next cage. She would beat at her chest with her fists, slap her face, yank at her hair, and throw what she tore out into the air.

Later, she would just cry, her tears rolling quietly down her cheeks. She would mop them up with her handkerchief, then wipe her nose.

But the thing I had seen in her eyes the first time did not change. It grew. And with it, my fear of her grew.

And, at the same time, her power over the two guards grew stronger. Their fear of her grew until her every wish became their command.

Who were those guards? What did they want? Why did they behave this way? So many questions were impossible to answer.

As for her relationship to them, I was very comfortable with it. I didn't feel for a second that the three of them formed a unit against me. Once, she scolded them in front of me, and they were shattered. She turned them to ashes, into two crawling insects. So they crawled. And she signaled them to get up after having almost crushed them underfoot. So they got up. And once again they were human guards, as before, like all other guards.

I can even say that her relationship with them was one of hostility. But I could never understand her hostility towards them, its reasons—and the motive behind it.

I also noticed that her hostility grew with the growing roundness of her belly. I felt protected. Even if they meant me harm, they wouldn't touch me without her permission.

The vague feeling grew within me that the longer she held me, the more necessary I became for her. With every passing day, giving me up became more difficult for her. I saw it in her eyes every time she entered the tent, every time she approached me, crouched before me, and glared at me with eyes flaring resentment and anger.

But why? Why did she resent me when I was innocent of her man's blood and had been innocent of all blood since the day I reached puberty? I hadn't killed anyone since my teens. I am innocent, innocent of her husband's blood. I didn't know him and didn't know anything other than what I'd read in the newspapers. Even the newspapers didn't mention the name of the killer. How could she accuse anyone? Especially me. I knew nothing and didn't read about it anywhere. I who, ever since my childhood, have always been terrified of being the one who had committed an unsolved crime.

Ever since I became acquainted with fear, I've been afraid of being the one whom no one could account for.

My fears were legitimate.

The unknown killer was me. She was certain of it. She had captured me for revenge. Killing me was my just due. It was the eye, it was the tooth.

After I tried to strike her back, after the guards shot at me and I fell to the ground, the blood dripping from the root of my arm, the pain became unbearable. I was trying the impossible, to control myself, trying not to scream so that she wouldn't take pleasure in my pain, the way her husband's killer had taken pleasure in his pain. At the same time, I was careful not to be too quiet, because then she would think that I wasn't hurting and order the guard to shoot me again. Or she could have left me alone until the next morning, to spend the whole night hemorrhaging. I was in a difficult situation. I had to do something, even when I knew that anything I tried might turn out for the worst. I decided to pass out. So I passed out. After a few seconds or minutes, I came to. I kept fading in and out of consciousness until I found myself in the emergency room, flung on a stretcher. I was being put through an intensive session of painful questioning to which I responded very briefly.

But they didn't ask for my opinion about the more important matter.

The matter of taking my arm from me.

They took my arm from me, uprooting it at the shoulder. They didn't ask for my approval. I was in a rage. I wanted to kill them all, the doctors, the nurses, the hospital workers, everyone. But my arm was already gone. My rage could not be calmed. And my arm's rage would not be calmed until they listened to me and returned it.

So they returned it to me.

They wanted to bury it, to put it to rest like a corpse.

Despicable.

They returned it to me to save themselves from my anger. I would have brought the hospital down on the heads of the nurses, the patients, and the bodies in the morgue.

At that time, they didn't understand my insistence on getting my arm back. They didn't understand it later either. They will never understand. To them, it's just a technicality. To them it's a question of whether it's possible to reattach it or not: if it's possible it should be done; if not, amputation is necessary, then a burial.

No.

I'm not talking about technicalities for God's sake. The issue is that it's my arm, and I have the right to have it by me. Connected or disconnected, I can't see myself without it, the five fingers, the nails, the soft fingertips, the skill and freedom of the fingers, the lines of age, of the heart, the future, the possible, and the impossible.

How could I give up my arm when it was taken away from me? Where would I be without my arm? Where would my arm be?

I had ignored my left arm so that my right arm wouldn't feel betrayed. I no longer use my left arm so that the right won't feel neglected.

No loyalty will surpass my loyalty to my right arm. I won't give it up no matter what people say, no matter what people think. My right arm first, my right arm second. My right arm until the very end. Nothing will happen without my saying so. My arm will remain at my side and no one will bury it.

Despicable.

But they did return it to me in the end.

No one can imagine how angry I was when they wanted to take my arm away from me and bury it in the ground. But they returned it to me. I stretched it out and put it in place along my right side, and tied it to my torso. It was the same as it had been, accompanying me wherever I went, wherever I reached, however I moved. I took an oath to protect it as I protected the pupils of my eyes.

The super visited me at the hospital, accompanied by the woman in mourning. He came in first and she followed bashfully. She was pregnant. That was the first thing I noticed after her black clothes— or maybe at the same moment. She was pretty, young, and in mourning.

After the "good-to-see-you" and after a moment of awkward silence, the super, directing his words to me, said that this woman was living in my apartment with her son. That way, he said, no gangster and no refugee from the shanties of South Beirut would take it over. He said she was looking after the apartment and my things, keeping the place clean. And looking after the trust. As he spoke, she gazed at the floor. She rarely raised her eyes towards me. And when she did, it was with great shyness. She was beautiful, young, widowed, in mourning, and pregnant.

The super added that his cousin, her brother-in-law, was also living in the apartment. The man's presence, he assured me, would guarantee that no one would take over the apartment.

I didn't answer. I was unable to talk or to think. I was, among other things, still recovering from the shock of my injury and amputation.

I was also under the influence of sedatives and sleeping pills.

I didn't stay in the hospital long. The wounded came in by the dozens. There were battles on the streets of the capital and at the southern border. The random shelling was occasionally hitting residential areas and resulting in numerous casualties. The chief surgeon visited me and told me that I was now well enough to leave the hospital.

The next morning I got dressed, put my right arm into the shirtsleeve, and left. But no sooner had I walked out of the hospital than I was nauseated, short of breath, dizzy. I broke into a sweat. I would have fallen, but I was determined not to give in... I walked a few more steps, then stopped to hail a taxi to my apartment. But the city was deserted. Explosions echoed from the front lines. Death was hanging in the air. There was no point in waiting. I realized that I had to walk. There was no other solution, really, no other option. I walked on, deliberately. My apartment wasn't far from the hospital, just a twenty-minute walk. Unexpectedly then, my lungs opened up and I could breathe deeply, unhindered. Feeling well again, I relaxed. I also relaxed because the streets were empty. Fearing the random shelling, people had disappeared into supposedly safe places... I relaxed because in circumstances like these there are no checkpoints where people crossed or disappeared, depending on their IDs.

But the echoes of gunfire from the front and of explosions from the residential quarters reminded me that I was still in danger. A shell could hit me at any moment. I could be killed or injured coming back home from the hospital.

I slipped my key into the lock. I froze. I listened. There was a strange sound, and the source of it was my apartment. It was an unfamiliar sound. At first I thought it was coming from the adjacent apartment. Then, realizing that the source of it was my own place, I panicked. I took the key out of the lock and hurried downstairs to the foyer. I waited for five minutes, convincing myself that it was just an illusion...that what I'd heard was nothing unusual. It must have been the neighbors. I decided that it was an illusion because I could remember times when I felt that there was a terrifying movement in the apartment, only to discover later that it was a figment of my imagination... The apartment would turn out to be empty.

I went back upstairs and opened the door. I entered confidently, unconcerned about the stirring around coming from the next apartment. As soon as I closed the door behind me, my eyes fell upon the young, pregnant, pretty woman in mourning. I panicked. I froze. I looked around me to make sure I wasn't in the wrong apartment. I wasn't. I was in my apartment, no doubt about that. The things were my things, the amount of light in the place was the same amount of light entering my apartment at this time of day, and the white of the walls was the same as that of my apartment. The cracks in the tiles at the entrance, the light switch to the right of the front door next to the old black phone, the light bulb hanging from the ceiling at the entrance. I recognized everything around me. Everything was mine. I'd bought it with my own money.

She panicked too. She froze in her place, not knowing what to say or do. Her confusion was obvious from her face and her hands, which were frozen in mid gesture.

She stayed frozen for a few seconds, then a few seconds more. But she couldn't hold out forever. After all, I was in my own house, among my own things, and the things in my house were mine. If I had said that to her, she couldn't have said anything else.

I wished I could breathe life into her, make her talk.

I waited.

Stupidly enough, I waited for my things to step forward and announce their loyalty, so the woman would know that it wasn't her house and that she was surrounded by things she didn't own. But my things let me down. They remained fixed and neutral. They stood deaf and dumb. They seemed not to mind this violation of ownership—this assault.

I looked at her again with the intention of explaining... and she called her son. There was a knock on the door. I turned around and answered it. It was the super. Hello, he said, walking in. I didn't answer. Instead, I pointed with my eyes towards the woman, but realized that she had disappeared into her room with her son. The super started dividing the house among us. The woman was to stay in the big bedroom with her son, I was to stay in the other bedroom, and the brother-in-law was to stay in the living room. He said he was sure that this situation wouldn't last very long, that there would be peace, and that everyone would be able to return to their homes. He said good things were in store. A Government of National Reconciliation had been formed, the first government since the beginning of the war to include all the country's various factions. Then he whispered in my ear that my guests wouldn't stay for long; even if the war didn't end, they were returning to their houses as soon as the shelling of South Beirut subsided.

He did reassure me.

Before he went out, he called his cousin's wife and told her that the Israelis had cut the road south, and that her brother-in-law wouldn't be able to return until they re-opened it.

The widow poked her head through the opening in the door, listening to Abu Ali. When he was done she backed her head in and closed the door, disappearing into the room.

Then the super left.

I went into my bedroom and lay down on the bed, my arm and me. I raised my eyes to the ceiling and pondered its whiteness, the shadows moving over it, and a large mosquito.

The mosquito was large and clearly visible; even its shadow was distinct against the white ceiling. It was the color of dust, its legs stuck to the wall, its back arched.

Its legs were long and slim, but each was sturdy in its own right. The arch of its back reminded me of the back of a camel, the back of a mountain.

It wasn't aware of my presence, or else it was just distracted by something.

Was it asleep?

Or had it fled to the ceiling, out of my reach, waiting for my movements to calm down before assaulting me?

I fell asleep though I didn't want to. I was still under the influence of the sleeping pills and sedatives.

A little past noon I was awakened by a soft knock at the door. I guessed the time from the bright light coming into the room. Half-awake, half-asleep, I asked:

"Who is it?"

No one answered, and things became muddled to me. For a moment, I thought I was at the hospital, that the people knocking were my parents. But how were they able to find me? Then I remembered that I lay wounded in my own house. It was the woman who had knocked at the door.

I don't remember what she said or whether she said anything, but her voice was friendly, shy, and hesitant. I got up and answered the door, but she had already left. So I stood at the door, trying to discern her movements. I went out of my room to find out where she had gone. I put my ear to her door and listened, hoping to detect some movement. I couldn't hear anything. She had placed a tray of food on the table in the living room and left with her child.

Probably to the super's apartment.

Certainly to the super's apartment: she didn't know anyone else in the building, on the block, or in the whole region.

On the tray there was a loaf of bread, a small plate of black olives in oil, a medium plate of raw *kibbeh* with some mint leaves on the top, an onion cut into four, and some oil. I ate a few olives without bread. I wasn't hungry. And besides, I don't like raw meat.

I got up and walked to the living room. I sat on a couch, looking at the furniture, and smoked. I fell asleep at some point and woke up to the noise of the woman and her child coming in. She opened the door and told him to come in first. He came in and she followed him inside. Since the main door opened on the living room, she came in to find me lying in front of her on the couch. She was surprised and tried not to wake me. But I had awakened and was sitting up. I was about to do something—I didn't know exactly what. But then she closed the door behind her and disappeared into her room, pushing her son in front of her. So I got up from the couch, went to my room, and locked myself in. I lay down on the bed and listened, trying to follow what she was doing in the next room.

She opened her door and went to the dining room to take away the tray and discovered that I had eaten only a few olives and that I didn't like raw meat. She carried the tray to the kitchen and washed and dried it, then put it in its place on the shelf. She threw the olive pits into the garbage and hesitated over the raw meat. The power was off, so she couldn't store it in the refrigerator. She emptied it into a skillet and fried it. Then she went to her room, called out to her son playing on the balcony and asked him to stay there. She asked him not to make any noise because she needed to get some rest.

She didn't take off anything except her shoes.

She lay on her left shoulder and raised her thighs to make a right angle with her back. She bent her knees, bringing her heels close to her bottom, and slept.

Her dress was thin and loose. She wore a slip beneath it so that it wouldn't be revealing.

She slept for a long time. Then she woke up, propped herself up on her elbows and, rolling over onto her bottom, she turned until she was sitting on the edge of the bed. She waited for a moment to wake up completely... I slept, still under the influence of the sleeping pills and sedatives.

I woke to a knock on my bedroom door. I got up quickly, trying to open it before she could disappear. But when I opened the door, she was gone. She hadn't left the house this time, as she had in the afternoon. She had gone to her room, closing the door behind her. What did she want, then? Why did she wake me up?

I left my room and wandered around the house, just as I had done that afternoon. There was a cup of coffee on the small table in the living room. Steam was still rising from it, its beautiful aroma filling the room. How I love the smell of coffee. But I wasn't supposed to take any stimulants, so the sleeping pills would work.

In spite of that, I sat on the couch, lit a cigarette, and took several sips of the coffee. I sat there, finishing the first cigarette, then lit a second and finished that too. After that, I returned to my room and closed the door behind me without locking it. I lay on my bed staring into space. The sun was setting and my room was getting dark.

The heat was increasing and everything was still. Sweat glistened on my body and I felt smothered, suffocated.

I usually go out at that time of day and don't return until the sun has gone down, until darkness has settled and light and shadow mix equally. But I couldn't get out of the apartment. I should go out to the balcony, I thought. It's spacious, has a commanding view and a comfortable rocking chair. Before opening my bedroom door, I stood behind it to discern her movements. After locating her, I left my room and crossed the distance between my bedroom and the balcony. When I thought it was safe to cross, I opened the door a crack and first poked my head out—just to make sure that she was out of sight. I heard a knock at the front door. So I retreated quickly into my room, closing the door before she could come out and answer. I lay on my bed, and could overhear the crowd.

"How are you?" "How are things?" "How's your health?" "Thank God you're safe!"

I got up and locked my door, then settled into my bed as they settled into the living room.

The heat in my room was murderous. It was as if the air were contracting. My arm was hurting, and I was out of breath, like someone walking around with a mountain on his back.

Not long after the visitors showed up, there was another knock at the door. I got up to answer the door, then I remembered that I wasn't supposed to. This time it was the super's wife. There was another commotion and the same exchanges were made. I thought that the meeting was going to remain in session, that I was going to be locked in my room all night, forever... But the super's wife invited them all down to her place, and they went.

They were all women except for a few boys and girls. They all went down to the super's place, including my apartment-mate and her son. I sighed with relief. The breeze came up and the air cooled. The light grew brighter and the shadows clearer; they became distinct again. After making sure that the house was empty of any people—living or dead, I left my room for the balcony and sat on the rocking chair. First, I lay back there, relaxing, then I went to the kitchen, drank some water and went to the bathroom to do my business. Going back to the rocking chair on the balcony, I rocked myself calmly and smoked. I contemplated the passage of time on one of the streets in Beirut.

I didn't feel the time passing when she was away. When she came back, it was as if she had only been gone for a second. I noticed that I'd left my bedroom door open. I didn't panic. I waited to see her reaction.

I could see her from the balcony carrying a lit candle. She had lit a candle in the kitchen, another in the living room, and another in her bedroom.

She was alone.

She moved carefully around the house, trying to find me. She was confused. I was nowhere. When there was only the balcony left to search, she approached it with the lit candle in her hand. Her eyes found me.

She panicked and shot back to the kitchen without saying a word. She turned around quickly, blowing out the living room candle on her way to the kitchen. There, she rattled the utensils irritably.

What was it that annoyed her?

I heard a commotion from the stairs. It came closer, so she hurried to my room, took the key out of the inside of my door, and locked it. She opened the door for the visitors. They had agreed to have dinner at her place.

At *her* place.

Because *I* didn't invite anyone to dinner.

Since the kitchen is large, she sat them in the kitchen, claiming that it was less bother that way.

The evening darkened and the fighting echoed from the front lines. It was amazing how quickly the streets were emptied. There was nothing left that would make anyone want to stay out. The visitors were quick to finish their dinner and leave. She saw them out, then closed the door even before the last of them had disappeared from her sight. She locked it and left the key in the lock, after turning it right—or left. She went back and lit the living-room candle.

Then she went to the kitchen where her son was slow in finishing his food. She made him hurry because it was bedtime.

At this time, I crossed the living room to my bedroom. But my door was locked.

She was surprised to hear me trying to open my door. She heard me rattle the knob, insist, fail, and start over again. It was confusing to me. I started wondering whether my left hand was failing me. She rushed towards me, took the key out of her pocket, unlocked the door, shoved it open, and returned to her son.

As soon as I closed the door, a thick darkness settled into the room. I had to grope my way to the bed. No sooner had I stretched out on it than the door opened without a knock. It was her, bringing me a lit candle. I rose, my heart rising with me. I found no words. I took the candle from her silently. She was silent too. But she had brought me the candle.

I put the candle on a small table near my bed. I lay down again, starting to feel the pain that I had been resisting in order to follow her and her son's movements. She was hurrying him along. She put an end to his dallying, told him to wash himself quickly, take his clothes off, and get into bed.

She was tucking him in with the white sheet from the closet when there was a knock on the door. She pulled the sheet up and ordered him not to move and to go to sleep. She went to open the door. It was the super.

She didn't open the door all the way. She opened it just a crack and stood blocking his way.

The super had come to ask how she was, to see whether she needed anything. He remained at the threshold, not trying to get in. She wouldn't have allowed it in any case. But she thanked him and said she was doing fine and that she didn't need anything. He

asked her about me and she said I had locked mysen ...
and didn't show myself to anyone. He nodded his head like some
one whose expectations had been confirmed. Then he left, and she
locked the door behind him. She left the key in the lock after turning it a little to the right—or to the left. She went back to the kitchen
to do the dishes, clear the table, and sweep the floor. She went to
the bathroom, then returned to the living room. She lay back on
the big couch, putting her feet on the small table where the cup of
coffee still sat.

She almost knocked over the coffee cup as she put her feet up
on the table. She almost knocked it onto the floor.

He didn't drink his coffee, she thought as she carried the cup
to the kitchen. He's had nothing to eat all day and nothing to drink.

She lay down in the living room again, relaxing, not thinking
about anything. It was hot, and her black clothes made it worse.
She got up to take off her clothes and put on her nightgown. She
got up to wash herself. The water wasn't running, but she was the
kind of woman who always planned ahead. She had stored some
water in a bucket.

In her bedroom, she took off her black dress and laid it carefully on a chair with the top of the dress draped across the back of
the chair. She took off her shoes and her black stockings, which she
later took to the bathroom with her.

She took out her nightgown from the closet. (She had hung her
clothes next to mine, in the same closet.) She carried it on her fore-
arm, preparing for her return from the bathroom.

While she was taking her clothes off, the door to her room
wasn't completely closed. She made the necessary preparations be-

hind the door, conscious and alert all the while. Nothing would take her by surprise. As for me, I was lying down, my door closed.

Nevertheless, she locked the bathroom door behind her.

When she crossed the distance between her bedroom and the bathroom, she was practically naked. A white bra covered her breasts, and the slip covered her from the waist to the knees.

She took off her slip, then took off her bra and hung it over the slip. She slipped off her panties and left them on the floor after moving them with her foot out of the way.

She stood in front of the mirror at the sink. She raised the candle to breast level and examined her body in the mirror, especially her breasts.

Soft breasts, a little saggy at the bottom, pendulous. Was her youth gone? Were the days of firmness gone? A son and a pregnancy and in spite of that her body still kept a lot of its freshness and firmness. Her shoulders were still straight, her skin soft, and her face beautiful; her eyes were wide and slightly almond shaped, and her nose was straight, stopping above the middle of her upper lip. Her nose was a good distance from her upper lip. Her lips were straight and full. When she smiled, her smile was so broad you thought it filled the place. Her chin underlined the roundness of her face. Her black mane hadn't lost a single hair. Her skin was olive-brown.

She brought the candle closer to her nipple. She gazed at it directly, without the mirror as mediator: she was a little irritated...a son, and soon another, and each time she would nurse for a year...

She brought it close to her other nipple.

She lowered the candle a bit, bending at the waist to follow its progress. She lowered it and stopped at her midriff.

As for me, I was surprised to find myself with an erection in spite of all the sleeping pills and the sedatives.

She stopped at her center where the triangle of hair did not respect its geometrical boundaries and overflowed in all directions. She bent down all the way in order to look at it, because her belly was swollen.

Her thighs were slender but full. She likes her legs a lot and takes care of them. The crimson nail polish is still on her toenails. She'd stopped polishing after her husband died in order not to expose herself to rumor. The truth is, ever since her husband died, she hasn't cared about the covered parts of her body.

Before she went into mourning, she used to comb the hair at the bottom of her stomach, at the cusp of her thighs and belly. She plucked the hairs that grew outside the triangle and bathed her body with raw olive oil before taking a shower. She would pass her hand over it, pressing lightly, smoothing her skin. She also shaved her underarms regularly.

She raised the candle to the level of her eyes and contemplated them for a long time, clutching her breasts in her other hand. She put the candle at the edge of the sink, moved to the bathtub and stood there, washing herself. She picked up the bowl of water and turned around to reach for her sponge, but remembered that she wasn't in her own house surrounded by her own things. Without hesitating for long, she took my sponge, and without hesitating at all, she wet it, worked up a generous lather, and soaped herself. She shuddered when the wet, cold, soapy sponge touched her body, even though the bathroom was very hot. She continued calmly after rushing through the first shock of it, lathering her whole body, then pouring water over it. She lathered her body again, pausing at length at her underarms. She also paused beneath her belly, between her thighs. She scrubbed. She scrubbed again. Once more. Up and down. Up and down. In an arching motion, from the top of her stomach and ending at her bottom. Finally, she poured water over herself, rinsing off everything that clung to her body.

She took the towel hanging on the doorknob. It took a deft maneuver to reach it: she stood on tiptoe, bent over, and stretched, trying to reach the towel without dirtying her feet on the floor. Carefully, she dried her front, her underarms, her private parts, and between her toes; then she wiped her ears with a cotton swab. After drying herself, she realized that she had forgotten the expensive bottle of perfume she'd used during her first meetings with her husband, before their marriage and after. She hadn't been using it but she had kept it hidden in a place where it wouldn't be found by anyone. It was in the closet with her underwear. From time to time she would come across it while tidying her clothes. She would take it out, contemplate it, and within her would awaken a mysterious desire of another kind. She would grow short of breath and return it to its hiding place.

She hadn't forgotten this perfume bottle when she'd deserted her house and taken only the bare necessities from what had survived the shelling.

After toweling herself she realized that she had forgotten the perfume bottle. But she soon remembered that she didn't need it and wondered why she remembered it when there was no man on the horizon.

She held her nightgown up to her body. Then she put it on. After tidying the bathroom quickly, she went to her bedroom. "The poor guy has had nothing to eat or drink. He's going to die of hunger if this goes on." She said that as she passed my bedroom door.

She lay down on her bed for a few moments, then stretched over to blow out the candle. There was darkness for a few moments, but light soon sifted in from the crack under the door. When she realized that she hadn't blown out the candles in the rest of the house, she gave herself some time before rising, then got up, and blew out the candle in the bathroom. Then the candle in the living room. Then she went to the kitchen candle where she remembered that she hadn't given me any dinner, that I hadn't had anything to eat or drink, so she sat down thinking. But a knock at the door interrupted her thoughts. She wondered who it could be at this late hour. It was nine o'clock.

Who could it be other than her brother-in-law? A choking feeling grabbed my throat. But if it had been her brother-in-law, he would have opened the door without knocking.

She got up and opened the door for the super. He'd come to tell her that the road from the south was still cut off, that her brother-in-law wasn't returning that night, and that she shouldn't hesitate to ask for his help if she needed anything.

When she had opened the door with her left hand, the draft almost blew out the candle she carried in her right hand. The flame was disturbed..

When the flame was disturbed, for a moment, she hadn't been able to make out the man at the door. Then she relaxed when it turned out to be the super. He greeted her before the flame had calmed down, and she knew him from his voice. She stood in his way at the crack of the door. His eyes slipped from her face to her neck, her chest, then the tops of her breasts. Then they slid even lower and she remembered that she was naked under her transparent nightgown. So she thanked him quickly, reassured him that she would be fine, and closed the door. He turned to leave but as she locked the door, he asked her about me. She said I was always in my room and never came out. He nodded his head like someone whose hopes had been dashed.

She locked the door, leaving the key in the lock after turning it a little to the right—or to the left. She went to the kitchen, thinking again about my resistance to food and drink. She blamed herself for not giving me dinner. She got up immediately and prepared dinner: *labneh*, olives, and a loaf of bread. She gave me the food and disappeared, the kitchen candle still lit.

I waited for her to go to her room before I started eating. I wanted to take the dish outside and eat on the balcony.

I didn't have to wait for long before hearing her bedroom door close. I went out, after making sure that all of the candles were out, and that no light sifted from beneath her door, that there was no movement. I walked out slowly, careful not to bump into anything.

I walked out barefoot, feeling my way. The light on the balcony allowed a general view of things. I put the dish on the small table, which I had bought especially for this spot. I sat on the rocking chair eating slowly.

The street was haunted by something. This something was alone, without a man, a woman, a fiend, a janitor, a car, or a bicycle. I could only sense a few rats and mice, even though I couldn't see them.

And the echoes of intermittent fighting at the front.

I was thirsty, but getting a glass of water was a complicated process, so I endured my thirst.

… And she came to me. Single, young, beautiful, almost naked, barefoot, olive skinned, carrying in her hand a glass of water, and in the other a lit candle. She walked towards me, holding her hand steady, careful not to spill the water.

I surprised myself with these hallucinations. I continued eating and I tried to forget about my thirst, contemplating the passage of time on one of the streets of Beirut, listening to the silence, which was interrupted from time to time by the echoes of periodic gunfire at the front, or the occasional lone explosion.

Then I did hear something. It came from my own apartment. It must be her brother-in-law, returning this late to take his brother's wife by surprise. My heart pounded. I felt a sharp pain in my right shoulder. I had to fight the need to throw up. Then I saw a light coming from within, approaching, illuminating the things it touched, casting long, dark shadows.

Could it really be him? Could he be coming from within? How had he come in without my knowledge?

... I closed my eyes and surrendered to whatever was to come.

I kept my eyes closed for a few moments, maybe a few hours. Maybe I fell asleep and was awakened by the light which had now disappeared. Everything was as it had been. It was dark inside. It was perfectly quiet. Outside, the darkness was diluted by a feeble light, the silence broken by periodic gunfire or the occasional lone explosion. Again, the street was haunted. Again, I contemplated it. This something was alone, without a man, a woman, a fiend, a janitor, a car, or a bicycle. I could only sense a few rats and mice, even though I couldn't see them.

It wasn't late yet. It was around eleven o'clock. I could tell from the weight of the darkness and the silence of the city air. But who was it, walking around the apartment? Could it be him, even though she had left the key in the door after locking it, just to prevent his surprising her?

Or did she forget to turn the key a little to the right—or a little to the left? I tried to search the living room from my place on the balcony but the darkness was too thick. I remembered then that I hadn't locked my bedroom door behind me. I was afraid that her brother-in-law had noticed this. So I got up immediately, carrying my dish to the kitchen with my left hand. I felt my way with extreme caution, careful not to bump into anything and make a noise that would wake her brother-in-law... Suddenly, it was as if I had been electrocuted. She lay before me, stretched out on the long couch. My wound reopened and the blood gushed. I dripped with sweat and the dish almost slipped from my hand.

She sat up!

I froze in my place, not knowing what to do. I hesitated. Looking at her there, I had some ideas. My emotions struggled with each other, but then she got up and walked towards me.

If only my right arm had been working...

She took the dish from me and brought it to the kitchen. I stood there not knowing what to do. I was thirsty. I was afraid that if I spent the whole night without water, I would die of thirst. So I followed her into the kitchen.

She was sitting there covering her ears, as if she had a headache.

She jumped when she saw me. Now she was on her feet, screaming. She screamed so loud that the dishes and pots shook. Recovering herself, she brought her hand to her mouth and cut herself off in mid-scream. She fixed her eyes on my shoulder where the wound had opened and the blood was pouring out. Again I could feel the water, the need for water, the thirst. My tongue had dried out and was thick in my mouth.

But how could I tell her that?

Her son had been awakened by her scream. He was up and crying. She went to him and soothed him back to sleep. And I stayed at the threshold of the kitchen, not knowing whether I was supposed to wait or go back to my room.

But could she leave me there, hemorrhaging?

Her son told her that he'd seen his father, that he had scolded him for disobeying his mother. He asked his mother whether she had told his father that he had disobeyed her. She said she hadn't. He asked her to tell him, if he asked again, that he'd been good. She promised she would, and he fell asleep, reassured.

The boy slept and his mother stayed at his side. I waited at the threshold of the kitchen, the blood oozing from the wound, soaking my clothes, almost reaching the floor.

I had to drink something. Otherwise I would fall down and pass out. Her son was asleep, reprimanding his dad now in the sunshine on one of the streets in South Beirut, where they once had lived. His dad was warning him to play in the shade so that he wouldn't get sunstroke.

Water. My lips were dry. My tongue was dry. Even if I had wanted to speak, I wouldn't have been able to. Blood ran from the wound in my shoulder while she knelt at her son's bed, playing with his hair. Her son had fallen asleep a long time ago. He was playing in the shade of some building, happy, after getting his dad's approval.

She remained kneeling at her son's bed, brushing his hair back with her fingers so that it stood erect on the top of his head before falling back into place. The stroking of his hair coaxed the boy to sleep. He slept peacefully. His father was kissing him for being good.

I struggled with confusion and hesitation, and they struggled with my thirst, the dryness of my tongue and the hardening of my lips, until the father of the boy came out, approached me with calm anger and reached into my mouth. He took out my tongue and replaced it with a piece of wood in the shape of a tongue. Then he broke off my lip, threw it into the garbage can and disappeared into the darkness. A woman appeared in his place, dressed in the white of a nurse. On her head was a nurse's cap, and in her hand a wire with a wet piece of cotton at the end. She put the wire into my mouth, and started swabbing my new tongue with it. The wood absorbed the water, and I stayed thirsty.

The thirst and my desire to drink grew. I felt I was going to die of thirst; I gagged and could hardly breathe. I was about to faint. I called out. I asked that the greatest doctor in the world be brought to me. He was contacted, but replied that he couldn't come because he was in the middle of emergency surgery. I asked that he be urged to come, that he be paid whatever he asked, but he kept refusing, and I kept insisting, until he felt sorry for me and came.

I was unconscious when he arrived. He gave the nurse orders I could not understand. She worked away until my lungs filled and my breathing returned. Finally, I regained consciousness and the doctor left. And the woman was still kneeling at her son's bed, brushing his hair back with her fingers, so it stood erect on the top of his head before falling back into place. The movement of his hair coaxed the boy to sleep. He slept peacefully. And I went back to pondering my motives.

She scolded him.

Suddenly.

She raised her voice a little and said to her son, "Go ahead and sleep. Enough." She went back to the kitchen.

She didn't seem to be surprised when she found me still standing at the threshold. She went in and sat in the same chair that she'd sat in with her head in her hands as if she'd had a headache. As for me, I was surprised. I was still very thirsty. She sat down. I went in search of water, turning things over, the nervousness of my actions increasing. I searched for a long time, so she rose calmly and said without moving, "What are you looking for?"

"I'm looking for water." I'm going to die of thirst. Who could have drunk the whole case of mineral water that I bought before I left and that I didn't get to drink a single bottle of?

"Where's the water?"

I said it forcefully, hitting an empty pitcher on the counter. It smashed into pieces and the youngster started crying. She rushed to him.

I still didn't have any water.

She knelt at his bed, playing with his hair, reassuring him with familiar words. I stood in the kitchen awaiting her return. But her son didn't respond quickly and didn't go to sleep as soon as I would have wished. So I sat in the chair she had sat in... I was still thirsty and my need grew with her son's reluctance to sleep. So I was filled with anger towards her. Why doesn't she just scold him and put an end to his whining? Why doesn't she just make him sleep?

My anger reached the point of exasperation. Then there was a knock at the door.

It was a light knocking, and it stopped. Then there was more light knocking.

She didn't hear it the first time, but she got up to answer the second time. She took the kitchen candle with her and closed the door behind her. She went to open the door. First she asked with a whisper, "Who is it?" Abu Ali answered that it was him. She didn't want to open the door, but his hand was quicker than her hesitation. He slipped through the crack and toward the living room, reprimanding her for not asking for his help.

He said that he'd heard her son crying and heard her moving around the apartment. He asked what had caused the racket and whether the boy was all right, said that he could get a doctor right away if necessary, that she shouldn't spare him when she needed help, that she was going through a difficult time, that people helped each other out during difficult times, and that it wasn't a favor but a duty.

Oh come now.

He asked her about me. She panicked. She said she had been sleeping and that she supposed that I was in my bed at this hour.

And when he began to assault her with questions, after settling back on the couch, she went back to her room without excusing herself, leaving it to me to sit with him and chat as if I were a host.

"The worst thing in the world is to be a super," Abu Ali said.

He wanted to continue in this vein, but he waited for me to get back from the kitchen first.

"I swear by God that when the war's over and when the Israelis pull out of the South, I'm going back to my home town to work the land. Be my own boss."

I took out another cigarette—the seventh, I think. I couldn't tell for sure because there were too many butts in the ashtray for me to count them easily. I offered him the cigarette. He took it from me, pulled out a match from his match box, struck it, and raised it to my face to light my cigarette. I hadn't pulled out my cigarette from the pack yet. So I had to pull one out quickly. He lit his cigarette and settled back into his seat.

"People think that a super sits on his ass all day long. If it hadn't been for me, this building would be crawling with refugees right now. During the Israeli invasion the summer before last, after everyone had run away, no one stayed here except me. My family left too. That gave me peace of mind.

"Every day some refugees would try to take over the building. Once, I had to shoot over their heads. One of them shot back at me. I would've died if I hadn't been lucky. It was only by a miracle that I survived.

"The most difficult job in the world these days is being a super. Your life's always in danger. With every new wave of refugees.

"Then the tenants come to you and treat you like nothing more than a super. And nothing more than that."

It was nearly sunset. The power would be out until midnight, according to the rationing plan. Darkness had been padding around the house for some time now, ashes emerging from the dimming light. The light seeping in from the outside through the window wasn't enough to separate the shadows. I was overcome by the desire to sleep. And drowsiness weighed heavy upon my moist eyelids and body.

"No one feels for you," the super said in a loud voice, getting up. "No one feels for you," he repeated even louder. "I could take advantage of my position if I wanted," he said, touching the gun at his waist.

Here.

I.

Stood up quickly. I rose up with the help of my crutches, because I'd lost my leg in the explosion. They'd wired my car, and it exploded when I turned the ignition. The shrapnel tore off my leg immediately. Pieces of it flew in every direction. Every part of it. The rest of my body didn't do well either. Very painful wounds. My blood flowed like sewage. My car was filled with it. It oozed out of me without anyone stopping to help. How could anyone over there help me, when they were the same people who'd planned my assassination?

When they thought that I was dead, they left the place. I was moved to the nearest hospital by a passerby. There—because I was dead—they put me among the dead. There were dozens of them and hundreds of casualties.

Hot spots in the city were on fire.

I was in the morgue, colder than I'd ever been before. I didn't have a name for it. It was enough to make me forget that I couldn't breathe.

She was the one who told me all about it. How they opened the boxes in the morgue, how they nearly gave up on finding my body; how when they finally found it, they identified it by my ring, which somehow hadn't been stolen and which had engraved upon it the first initial of the first woman to love me.

They panicked when they noticed I was still moving. They screamed that I was still alive. The place bustled with activity. Alarm spread among the people there searching for family members. There were demands that corpses be double-checked before being placed in the morgue. The drawers were reopened. But no other living corpses were found.

The super's wife was the one who told me all about this, when she came with her husband to visit me in the hospital. He wasn't saying anything, just smiling from time to time.

"You're quite a hero, Abu Ali," his wife said. As she told the story, she kept turning to him in admiration. Every time, he said something that meant, more or less, that life wasn't worth much if a man couldn't be there when somebody else needed him.

Ever since that accident, he's insisted that I not hesitate in asking him or his wife any favor. He always reminded me that his wife was a first-rate cook.

"I didn't want to be a bully," said Abu Ali.

I can never forget the way his wife handed me that glass of lemonade as I climbed the stairs to my apartment after returning from the hospital. I would take a swallow of it and she would take it from me. She would give it back to me whenever I climbed a step or two. I would take a sip and rest a little while Abu Ali, on the step below me, helped keep me steady. He consoled me, cursing war and its militiamen, He cursed weapons, those who make them, those who buy them, and those who use them.

"I didn't want to be a bully," he repeated.

He bent over and pulled out a cigarette from the pack. There were only a few left. He lit his cigarette, this time not handing me one. He smoked and wandered around.

The darkness deepened, erasing the shapes of things. It brought humidity and heat, expelled the air, and filled up the space where the air had been.

After putting out his cigarette, he disappeared for a moment and returned with a small carpet in hand. He spread it on the floor and started praying.

That was the first time I ever saw him pray.

What was going on? Why in my house and in my presence? What did he expect me to do while he prayed? What did he have planned for me this time?

I stood still.

He was immersed in his prayer, as if Divine Mercy was pouring over him from on high. He didn't bite off any of his prayers, didn't cut any of them short. When he stands, he stands with balance. When he kneels, he kneels deeply. When he bows, he stands still then bows fully. And when he lifts his head, he balances it, attaining perfect stillness.

But at the same time, he didn't exaggerate a single movement. He didn't hesitate before reciting the refrains, and didn't delay in rising, kneeling, or bowing.

When his prayer was finished, he got up, saddled his horse, and galloped away.

It was hot and humid, the darkness sultry. It was hard to keep my eyelids open. I wished I could sleep. I wasn't awake enough to fall asleep. And I wasn't really asleep enough to pull myself awake. Trapped in that space between drowsiness and sleep. Somebody once told me that in situations like this, the only option is to adapt. Otherwise, it becomes unbearable. The first step in adapting is to practice forgetfulness. Oblivion. Forgetfulness is to regard what happens to you as something that you can't control—no matter who you are. He advised that whenever there's gunfire in my neighborhood, I should wait, then carefully and stealthily look out the window and determine the location of the combatants and their line of fire to determine the best place to hide. That way you avoid getting wounded. Unless it happens by chance. Chance is something you can't predict, even during peacetime. When I asked Abu Ali how to deal with sectarian backlash, he advised me to be cautious. He said, "If a political figure has just been assassinated, don't go out of your house." Then I asked him what to do if the assassination took place—God forbid—while I was out, say… in my car, returning to my house or on my way somewhere, walking, running an errand, or just walking around undecided where to go… He got upset by my question, thinking that I was making fun of him. I swore that I wasn't, that this was a real concern of mine. I reminded him of the political leaders who had been assassinated and the chaos that had resulted from their parties' responses. When he calmed down, I asked him what to do in case they started breaking into houses to take revenge. He replied that this rarely happened.

My friend Hassan had another opinion. He said that I had to overcome my anxieties, change the decor of my house. He said that this was bound to help me forget and to take things more lightly. Or else, he added, I should leave the country. I was surprised by this. I thought for a long time before answering, "But where to?"

After finding a job and settling down in Beirut, Hassan was the first person I'd made friends with. We've been friends ever since, and I used to take him to my village when I visited. My mother loved him and noticed that he was very clean. She appreciated this quality of his and wondered how this was possible when he hadn't been baptized. If I hadn't scolded her, she would've asked him whom he'd learned his cleanliness from.

When he finished his prayer, Abu Ali reached down to his waist, pulled out a comb from his pocket, and combed his hair.

It was very hot and humid, the darkness sultry. Whenever anything touched me, I felt like it was sticking to me.

The water was off. It was summer. It was hot and the humidity made everything heavier. I remembered the river in my village, reflecting the sun, the children diving in and climbing out.

I panicked, imagining that Abu Ali was asking how I managed to find water to wash with. But my panic was soon absorbed by the drowsiness soaking into my tissues, into the cells of my brain.

Hassan, one of my best friends, didn't know yet that I was back. I hadn't gotten in touch with him.

He wants me to get married. For many reasons. One of them is that I am getting old, so old I might miss that train forever.

Hassan has been insisting that I get married for a long time. He grew more insistent the longer the war dragged on. His wife had an unmarried friend, who supposedly had all the qualities I could ask for in a wife. Lately, his pestering had become more than I could take. "How can I get married under these circumstances?" I said to him. "I'm in my house right now, but at any moment I might have to leave it."

"If the tenants had been from my own sect, I would've acted differently," said Abu Ali, "I would've given them the treatment they deserve. But I'm always afraid that things might be misinterpreted. I'm no sectarian. It's no difference to me whether a tenant is a Druze, a Maronite, a Sunni, or a Shi'ite. If I need help, none of them will offer it. I spent hundreds of liras when my daughter was ill recently. No one offered me a piastre. Do you know how much it costs these days, renting an apartment like this? Forty thousand liras. Forty thousand liras. You people are still paying the old rent of five thousand. Some people forget that if they lost their old apartments, they would never find a new place that they could afford. Not in a million years."

"Get married, my friend. Get married." Hassan insists.

The air reeked of spilled blood, and of the blood about to be spilled. In every district. In every building. In every apartment. On every street, of course under bridges, and in shelters. Everywhere.

The air reeked of blood, and I was in the middle of a nervous breakdown such as no one had ever experienced before me.

The air reeked of blood when Hassan said to me, "Have you considered changing your religion?"

My mother yanked me back.

I felt my mother grab me by the shirt tail; she yanked me so hard it made me shudder. My brother and niece were indignant. Church bells rang in my head. The giant chapel bell tolled. The church overflowed with the sound of hymns and chants as the rain drowned village alleys. Snow sat on the horizon. Tomorrow, it will reach our door.

Hassan didn't care about converting me. He wasn't religious himself. This was just his solution for putting an end to my fears.

He uttered the words and examined my face for some response, his eyes nearly overflowing with tears.

Abu Ali hadn't completed his first round of prayer before the devout souls of my village were being enflamed by the priest's words.

"Grant our kings victory, oh Lord, and deliver our enemies into their hands."

A grumble passed through the congregation, and the floodwaters were turned. Everyone knew what had happened the day before. Some didn't wait for the morning light. Some didn't wait till the prayers were done. They set out on treacherous paths, down steep valleys, with the winds over mountain tops, unafraid of death. What is death anyway, when it is in the name of truth, in the name of faith, and in the name of God?

He was a fearful knight, drinking the blood of his foe like running water. He slaughtered his enemy at the spring and, having no cup to fill, he cupped his hands and filled them with the blood that pumped from the aorta. After quenching his thirst, he wiped his mustache on his sleeve, and left with the blood on his clothes, having set an example in bravery. He'd taught them a lesson. They would not play with fire again. Never again would they toy with the sacraments, the sacred symbols, places, and objects of another people.

Our forces were able, in spite of our limited resources, to take possession of the fortified sites of the enemy.

Our heroes live eternally in heaven, even while their corpses lie still on the battlefield, scavenged by birds, devoured by worms.

The heat was suffocating. Things never despaired of being just things.

Before he got angry, Abu Ali was sitting on the couch opposite me. He stood up, and the couch didn't get up with him. The table also stayed in its place, unchanged, and so did the walls, the ceiling, and the floor.

But the evening dragged on. The temperature rose. The air became thinner in each square centimeter of the room. The humidity increased.

When he finished his prayers, Abu Ali waited a little before calling the widow. He waited for her to come back on her own, to tell him what was going on with her, to excuse herself at least. But she didn't come, so he went to her room. The door was closed, and he knocked lightly. She guessed that it was him, so she got up quickly, lest he wake her son. She opened the door and, without giving him a chance to talk, said, "What's the matter with you, Abu Ali?" She shut the door in his face, so that he would understand that he'd gone too far.

So Abu Ali left the apartment, and I was left alone in the kitchen. Once again she was alone with her son in her room. Once again, I was in pain. Once again, I was thirsty. Once again, I was bleeding. Once again, I silently pleaded. And, once again, she took her time coming back.

I was sure she wouldn't be able to go to sleep without doing something for me. She didn't go to sleep. But she didn't come either.

She was stretched out on her bed—her bed was my bed—and dreams seeped from her, but I couldn't catch any of them because of my thirst and my pain.

When I could no longer stand, I sat in the same chair she had sat in, waiting. Nothing had changed about it. It was still made of wood, with a backrest, a seat, a shape, and a color.

I lifted my foot to the seat, pulled my calf to my thigh, and rested my chest on my thigh and my chin on my knee. I hugged my shin and thigh with both arms—just as she had—so that my breasts were between my thigh, chest, chin, and knee. I squeezed. Then I released my leg. I was still leaning over so that they spilled, first right, then left; and obediently with all their weight my breasts moved with me. I sat up, and they came to rest, swelling beneath smooth skin that you would want to touch and that you would desire.

My long hair fell to my waist like spring ferns.

My legs stretched long and complete, meeting at something like a triangle.

I felt the urge, so I went out to the bathroom, groping my way carefully in the darkness. I sat on the toilet, a beautiful woman sitting on the toilet. I started peeing. I stood, pulling up what I had just slipped down around my knees. The dress I'd been holding up draped around me again. I returned to the kitchen without washing, waiting for the urge to pass. I was beautiful. Nothing escaped me, not even the effect of my beauty upon the people who lived in the house with me. I was determined not to be the source of conflict between any two people, especially between her and her husband. That said and, speaking frankly, if he hadn't been married, I would've married him. I would have fallen in love with him. I admit that I secretly wished that it were possible to be with him. To take him and be taken by him. I'm not saying she doesn't have reason to blame me. I understand her completely. I admit that all her behavior is justified. If I'd been her, I would have acted the same way.

But I'm not guilty.

I'm a lonely woman in this house. And the house is mine. She came with her husband to live with me against my wishes. They left their house against their will. Ever since they got here, her husband hasn't tired of looking at me. But he is very proper. Treats me with irresistible sensibility. I'm lonely in this place, young, and beautiful. My parents have left. I couldn't follow them and they couldn't come back. We can't all leave the house. He's a beautiful, brave, kind, and moral man. I'm reluctant to do anything that might be seen as provocative or inviting. Although I secretly love him, desire him, and dream of having him in my bed, I haven't told anyone about my secret or my dreams.

His wife sleeps, and I can't sleep. I envy her being able to sleep. Her husband is like me. He can't sleep either. Perhaps I'm the reason. But whatever the reasons, the result is the same for the two of us. He consoles me when I have insomnia; he takes away my fears. He reassures me.

But day by day, his wife began to turn into a dangerous woman. Jealousy has its own logic and wisdom. She would frown at me, be unpleasant to me. I used to forget about it, as if I didn't see or hear. I didn't tell her husband anything about it. He wasn't aware of anything. That's probably why he wasn't cautious enough.

I once overheard them fighting, screaming at each other. She threatened to kick me out of the house, and he threatened her in return—I don't know what with. He denied having a relationship with me, denied his desire for me. She wasn't convinced and asked her brother to help her. He would visit the house regularly. He would try to arouse my interest. He'd try to seduce me. He would invite me for a breath of air, just for a change. I accepted the first time, so that he would get to know me for who I am, so that he would trust me and keep his sister from mistreating me. For a while, I thought I'd succeeded. But I soon realized that I was wrong. Or rather, I soon realized that my success was only temporary, and soon it turned to failure. He started asking for more than a walk, and when I refused, he would pester me and become a nuisance. I was convinced that, in the right circumstances, he would rape me. I kept away from him. I avoided him and this angered him, even though I tried to make him understand that he could never be more than a friend. He became irritated. So irritated that he finally spat up what had been stewing inside him. He accused me of being his brother-in-law's mistress. I denied it. He accused me of destroying his sister's life and the life she'd been building with her husband for years. He threatened to destroy my reputation if I didn't behave myself from now on. When he realized that his threats weren't doing him any good, he threatened to kill me if I didn't leave the apartment.

"If you leave your house, the landlord will rent your apartment for forty thousand liras. Where do people like us get forty thousand? That kind of money doesn't grow on trees."

"Get married. I'm telling you, you should get married," he said, pushing her into my arms.

"But, Hassan. My name. What will my name be?"

"Get married and call yourself whatever you want. Just stay alive."

And so, my name changed to something I didn't want. I saved my neck by staying alive. When my mother heard about it, she carried her blankets and bed clothes to church and vowed to stay there day and night until I returned. She remained there, and I stayed away, and she pledged to fast day and night, and the news spread throughout the village, and she became ashamed to face people.

As for my father, he lost his mind. He tore off into the fields and didn't come back. He didn't make any vows or oaths. He was the one who had given me my name, the name of his father and great grandfather.

My father stopped going to church. He stopped praying. Whenever he heard the church bells tolling, he wouldn't know where to hide. He would sit in the shade somewhere and cover his ears with his hands for a long time.

My father decided to come to Beirut, even though roads were closed and the passage unsafe.

He decided to come to Beirut no matter what. He managed to arrive safely. When he knocked at the door, I knew it was him. I asked my wife not to answer, to go to the bedroom, not to come out until I said so. She stared at me, wide eyed. I raised my voice at her, telling her to do as I said. When she didn't move, I screamed and almost struck her. But she did go to the bedroom, closed the door, and locked it behind her.

Joseph!

I looked around me before embracing him. I was checking to see whether anyone was watching or listening. I threw myself into his arms, breathing in the smell of his sweat, the fields, the village, and the alleys. I decided to ignore the smell of church.

"Why didn't you come back, Joseph? You said you weren't going to stay here for long." Circumstances. Circumstances, Father.

How could I leave my apartment, my job? What would I be without them? "Your life is more precious than anything. Come, let's go. You'll stay with us in the village until this damn war ends."

My father was nearly seventy. He had his mountain pants on, a shirt which was white when he bought it, a navy blue jacket, and shoes that buckled at the ankle.

My father was dressed in his formal clothes. He wore them to church on Sundays and holidays, when visiting a notable, or on special occasions.

It was hot in Beirut. Sweat glistened on my father's face, as if he'd washed it and not dried himself. "Don't you want to see your mother?"

Changing names isn't going to solve the problem, Hassan.

Solving problems isn't our immediate concern. Our primary concern is your safety. Get married, and don't have kids right away. When the war ends, do as you see fit. When the war ends… "What if I get married without changing my name?" "Then you'd be adding to your problems and complicating things for your wife."

It would have been easier for me if I had been a woman. A woman changes her name anyway. She takes her husband's.

And the husband makes her have kids, whom she has to look after until they grow up to be like their father.

Abu Ali took a drag from his cigarette, pausing before he exhaled. "This government is useless," he said. "I don't expect anything to change. Consider the ministers one by one. Adel Osseiran. It's true he's a Shi'ite and the Minister of Defense, but everybody knows he's Chamoun's man. And Chamoun got the Ministry of Finance, so in other words he holds the key to everything. If any Minister proposes a project he doesn't like, Chamoun simply won't give him the money. He won't sign. What use is a Ministry without money? Chamoun is the money. The whole government is Chamoun's. I'm not hopeful. And the coming storm will be even worse, as always."

When I proposed a different solution to Hassan, he just smiled. He didn't disagree with my views. But my views still made him smile. He doesn't oppose my hopes for the future. He supports me in what helps for the present. I have to deal with the source of my anxieties right now. My dreams can't save me from the present. This dream of mine—its time has passed, or else it hasn't come yet.

"What if I could love you in your form of worship, and you love me in mine?" I said.

"Beautiful words, my friend, but I don't pray, and neither do you."

When he bowed, Abu Ali's head touched his little girl. She'd crawled over to where he was praying, and he opened his eyes to find her there. He kissed her, sniffed her gently, nuzzling her with one long breath, his eyes closed. He breathed her in until his lungs were full. Then he nudged her away with his head and continued praying. When he was done, he bowed, knees locked, hands at his sides. He looked at her, watched her, thoughtful. Then he took her in his hands, lifted her up, and pressed his face into hers. Kissing her, smelling her, holding his breath in. Then he put her back on the floor and went back to his seat.

Done with his prayers, Abu Ali sat on the couch, his face radiant. He pulled out a small comb from his pocket and combed his hair. He returned it to his pocket and sighed.

"Oof."

Haseeb says: "Why are you so afraid? There are thousands of Christians in West Beirut. Muslims are assaulted more often than Christians. Think about it. There are no Muslims left in East Beirut. They all had to leave. Not counting the family that was killed last week, no more than ten Christians have been killed since the sixth of February. Anyway, I'm not telling you that everything is fine with the country. We're still shaken by these sectarian outbursts—these massacres. These days it's only sensible to be cautious, not to go out at night, not to sleep alone in your house. If you can't be patient, move to another area. And I tell you this as a friend: don't tell people about your anxieties. You'll just be a nuisance. People have enough worries of their own. They don't want to have to deal with yours as well."

It was Abu Ali who opened the door when the knock came. It was the third, the fourth, or the tenth time that someone had knocked and Abu Ali had answered. But this time, he stayed at the door for a long time. I heard an exchange of words, but I couldn't make out what was said. Then he returned and settled back into his seat. When he saw my eyes, insistent on knowing who it was and what had happened, he said:

"Don't worry. Everything's all right. They're just kids."

My anxieties flared up. I had been badly wounded on the road from the Museum to Barbeer. Abu Ali's enemies had shot me. That was the place where I was wounded, closer to the Museum than to Barbeer. They'd left me there to bleed, until my blood reached the lip of the gutter. My blood flowed slowly, red over the black asphalt. I wished it could have run over the soil instead.

But what could I do if it was all meant to happen? What could be worse than watching my own blood being swallowed by the sewers of Beirut?

My blood was dark red, and it drew a map as it ran towards the lip of the gutter. Then a rat appeared. It must have come out from the place where my blood was pooling. It started drinking, then other rats joined it. They jostled with each other for my blood.

They left me to bleed until I'd been drained to the last drop, until my veins were dry, and my body became brittle as old wood.

When they were sure that I had died, with no hope of recovery, they moved me to the hospital where I was put into a box in the morgue—a corpse waiting to be identified.

But Abu Ali couldn't believe it when the radio mentioned my name among the casualties. He was terribly confused. He couldn't go to East Beirut. What could he do? Then it came to him. He stood up immediately and took off his clothes to shower. But the water wasn't running. He called to his wife and she gave him some of the water she had hoarded. He washed, and instead of putting on his own clothes, he dressed like a Christian. He stood at the mirror, combing his hair. Before leaving, he looked into his eyes. Probing their depths.

What did Abu Ali see in the eyes of Abu Ali? Why did he smile? What was the meaning behind this half smile of his? And who smiled first?

But this was no time for humor. When Abu Ali called his wife over, she came in but didn't recognize him. She almost asked him who he was, but he was quick to say:

"It's me. Abu Ali."

It was hot and humid, and darkness was gradually descending. You could feel the air get thinner in each square centimeter of the room. Sweat glistened on me like wet glue.

It was as if I was made of drowsiness. I could only open my eyes with great effort, only to close them inspite of myself.

The objects in the room, the furniture, had already lost their shadows. Now they were losing their shapes as well.

The street was empty, except for the occasional car, the odd pedestrian hurrying by.

It was a sultry evening. Sweat stuck to your body and soaked your clothes. I had to exert myself just to breathe, to get enough air.

If the humidity had been the subject of a news broadcast, it would have been described as extremely high, eighty percent or more. Ninety, even more, certainly.

There is an animal quality in the color of darkness. The dark came on slowly, as if emanating from every object in the house, through little pores invisible to the naked eye. It was in the fiber of the walls, among the threads of various fabrics. It went out through the window after dispersing in the space of the room, with the most precise vision, and an insistence which never waned or hesitated.

Whenever it descended, the darkness pressed against me, as if it could not settle in completely until it had chased me out.

I was right there.

Unable to fight it even with light. I longed to give in to sleep, to be rid of its nuisance.

But how could I, when Abu Ali kept reassuring me about the very source of my fears. "Don't worry. Everything's fine. They're just kids."

I could hear their shouting, their obscure conversation.

"Don't worry. Everything's fine. They're just kids."

Abu Ali's wife did not recognize him. He started unbuttoning his fly. Frightened, she ran away, barely suppressing a scream. She showed up at my place, asking for help. I rushed down with her to her apartment on the ground floor.

Abu Ali was naked in front of the mirror. He was looking down at himself first, then looking at his reflection in the mirror. It was the same person. And the person in the mirror was the same person who'd stood before his wife after taking the shower, the same person who gave that secret smile which he himself didn't understand.

When he felt our presence in the room, he turned around to look at us. He wasn't bothered by the fact that he was naked before us. He said to his wife:

"Umm Ali. Umm Ali. I'm Abu Ali."

She rushed over to him and handed him his clothes, saying:

"Abu Ali. When did you come in? Did you see that guy who was here sayin' he was you?"

"But I'm telling you, that was me."

"No. It wasn't you. It was somebody else."

Abu Ali slapped his forehead. He bent over, sobbing, holding himself as if he were wounded in the stomach.

"It's me, Umm Ali. Have mercy, it's me."

"No, you listen. Somebody was here sayin' he was Abu Ali, and he unbuttoned his fly in front of me."

"It's me. I'm telling you. It's me."

"It was somebody else," she screamed.

"It was me," he answered.

The screaming got louder and louder and finally subsided. Abu Ali crouched in one corner of the room, bent over as far as he could.

Umm Ali took the pins out of her hair and dropped on to the edge of the bed. She went limp; her knees gave way beneath her. She was stretched over the bed, twitching as if ants were crawling in her muscles and in her bones too.

Abu Ali stood in front of the mirror in a final attempt.

The person in the mirror was the same person who had been there after the shower.

He was still naked. He felt a chill then and realized he was naked. He hurriedly covered himself. Before putting his clothes back on, he looked at me. He looked at me hard.

"Look at me." He said. "Am I Abu Ali, or not?"

He paused, and said:

"They're playing games with me."

It was hot and humid, and the darkness was as I described it. It was sunset, and there was only one cigarette left in the pack. Abu Ali had it. He had the filter between his lips and opened the matchbox, but found it empty.

"Hard times..." he said. "Do you have a lighter?"

Abu Ali knows that I have a lighter.

"A lighter is better than a matchbox. It lasts longer."

Abu Ali knows that I have a lighter, and that it's gold-plated—a Ronson.

"But you must always be careful not to forget it somewhere. Otherwise, you lose it."

Abu Ali spoke with the cigarette between his lips, and the empty matchbox in his hand.

"Is your lighter out of fluid, then?"

So I reached into my shirt pocket and took out my lighter. I laid it on the table. He picked it up. We heard a new knock at the door. He got up to answer it as he lit his cigarette and slid the lighter into his pocket.

"Don't move. I'll answer it."

He stayed at the door for a long time. I could hear them shouting their obscure conversation. I heard the shouting grow louder, but I could only make out one sentence.

"We wanna come in."

I got up to get my sleeping pills and took a multiple dose. I collapsed on the bed and waited for the time to pass, for the pills to do their work.